# One Night with a Marine

A SINFUL MARINES NOVEL

Makenna Jameison

This book is a work of fiction. Names, characters, places, and incidents are the product of the author's imagination. Any resemblance to actual events, locales, or persons, living or dead, is coincidental.

Copyright © 2019 by Makenna Jameison

All rights reserved, including the right of reproduction in whole or in part in any form.

ISBN: 9781093628654

ALSO BY MAKENNA JAMEISON

## ALPHA SEALS

SEAL the Deal
SEALED with a Kiss
A SEAL's Surrender
A SEAL's Seduction
The SEAL Next Door
Protected by a SEAL
Loved by a SEAL
Tempted by a SEAL
Married to a SEAL
Seduced by a SEAL
Rescued by a SEAL

## SOLDIER SERIES

Christmas with a Soldier
Valentine from a Soldier
In the Arms of a Soldier
Return of a Soldier
Summer with a Soldier

# Table of Contents

| | |
|---|---|
| Prologue | 1 |
| Chapter 1 | 4 |
| Chapter 2 | 9 |
| Chapter 3 | 18 |
| Chapter 4 | 25 |
| Chapter 5 | 32 |
| Chapter 6 | 42 |
| Chapter 7 | 58 |
| Chapter 8 | 67 |
| Chapter 9 | 72 |
| Chapter 10 | 80 |
| Chapter 11 | 91 |
| Chapter 12 | 100 |
| Chapter 13 | 106 |
| Chapter 14 | 115 |
| Chapter 15 | 121 |
| Chapter 16 | 129 |
| Chapter 17 | 137 |
| Author's Note | 151 |
| About the Author | 153 |

# Prologue

The wind whipped colorful leaves through the air, and Amy Mitchell glanced up as she jogged along the wooded trail, watching them swirl around before landing on the path in front of her. Red maple leaves mixed in with shades of yellow and brown, covering part of the ground. In another week, the trees would be bare, leaving the landscape stark for the upcoming winter. But for now, at the peak of the season, she basked in fall's perfection.

She took a deep breath, inhaling the crisp air, and looked up to the clear blue sky that was peeking through the branches. This time of year always energized her—the hot summer sun had given way to fall, the air was cool and crisp each morning.

And after a day of teaching rambunctious preschoolers?

Nothing was better than a solitary afternoon run on the trails.

Her mind drifted, lost in the rhythm of her movement. There was the art studio she dreamed of opening someday, if she could ever save up the funds. The pies she needed to bake this weekend for the school bake sale on Monday. The preschool classes she taught. The new artwork she would paint to adorn her bedroom walls.

And always in the back of her mind, drifting into her subconscious thoughts when she least wanted it, was her ex.

The guy who couldn't settle down but got engaged to someone else right after Amy broke up with him. Although she'd known him forever, they'd dated only a few short months before she called it quits.

And the next thing she knew, *bam,* he was with another woman.

*Engaged* to someone else.

Occasionally she'd catch him glancing her way if they happened to run into each other when they were out, but she generally avoided him at all costs.

Tried to pretend it didn't sting that he'd gotten over her so quickly.

That he'd found someone else while she was one hundred percent single.

She sighed, trying to clear him from her mind as she continued to jog through the forest. It was better for both of them if she moved on. Obviously he had.

*Moved on. Moved on. Moved on.*

Her feet pounded on the trail.

She'd meet someone else. Another man would come along and sweep her off her feet. Kiss her senseless.

But until then?

She pounded out her frustration, picking up her

pace slightly as she jogged through the remaining stretch of path toward the parking lot. Perspiration beaded on her forehead, and she pushed herself harder, deciding to sprint back. Cranking up the music, she let the song that was blasting in her earbuds drown out any more thoughts.

There.

*Pound. Pound. Pound.*

Her feet hit the ground as she ran.

Cool autumn air filled her lungs.

It was like she hadn't even been thinking of him at all.

# Chapter 1

Marine Corps Captain Jason Patterson sauntered across the parking lot at Quantico, nodding as a junior officer saluted him. Rows and rows of cars filled the massive lot, the bright sunlight gleaming off of them. He glanced up at the clear blue sky, adjusting his sunglasses. His shift in schedule this week had thrown him off, but hell if he didn't love a chance to spend a couple of afternoons off base enjoying the damn perfect autumn weather.

Virginia fall days were a hell of a lot better than the long days he'd spent in Afghanistan, deployed with the Marines.

He shrugged his shoulders, letting some of the tension roll off of him. After years of deployments with the military, he still wasn't used to a desk job. Sitting in an office all day wasn't quite what guys like him were made to do, but hell. Training junior officers wasn't necessarily a bad thing. And moving around all the time from deployment to deployment got old pretty damn quickly. There was nothing wrong with being stationed so close to the nation's capital if it meant he could stay in one place for a while. Maybe put down some roots. Imagine what life could be like when he eventually left the Corps.

He clicked his key fob, the *beep beep* of his car alarm resounding across the concrete.

"Hey, Jason!" his buddy Tyler Braxton called out, walking toward him across the lot.

"How was the briefing at the Pentagon?" Jason asked, stopping midstride to wait for his friend.

"Boring as hell. But at least I beat some of the 195/Beltway traffic. I'm still not used to the shit show that's DC around rush hour."

Jason chuckled. "I doubt anyone ever gets used to that."

"You headed out already?"

Jason nodded. "Affirmative. I got here at oh-dark-thirty this morning. Next week I'm back on my regular shift."

"Well hell, maybe I'll catch up with you later then. I'll shoot you a text. Some of us are getting together for a couple of beers."

"Sounds good," Jason said. "I'd be up for that. Talk to you then."

After dropping his gear into the trunk, he climbed into his black sports car, turning the key in the ignition as the engine roared to life.

The shift in his schedule meant traffic wasn't too bad either, and he pulled into his neighborhood less than thirty minutes after leaving base. Neat little yards lined the welcoming street, and he pulled into his own driveway, already making plans for his run. He climbed out of his car and glanced up as he saw his neighbor pull in across the street, the tires of her silver SUV slightly muddy, with splotches of dirt spread across the lower part of her vehicle.

He thought she was a preschool teacher and wondered where she'd been all afternoon. Maybe they'd taken a field trip somewhere? Did preschoolers even take field trips?

He wasn't sure but then realized if they had taken a class trip, they'd most certainly have ridden on a school bus like all the other children did. It wasn't like she would be chauffeuring them around.

He watched as Amy stepped out of her SUV, wearing those tight, stretchy pants women wore when jogging and a snug tee shirt. A long-sleeved shirt was tied around her waist, and her long, brown hair was pulled back into a ponytail that swung back and forth as she moved.

She ducked back into her SUV and grabbed an arsenal of gear—some type of tote bag, purse, and a black gym bag. She glanced across the street but didn't seem to even notice him as she shut the door and walked toward her front porch.

Her hips swung as she walked, and he found himself wishing that she didn't have the shirt around her waist. With the way the rest of her body was trimmed and toned, he was sure she had a tight little backside.

Killer curves never hurt anyone.

She turned slightly, adjusting her bags as she fumbled with her keys, and he caught a glimpse of the swell of her breasts in that snug top.

So goddamn gorgeous.

Not that he needed to be chasing after his neighbor. No matter how attractive she might be.

Her house was identical to the one he was renting across the street, save for the fresh pots of yellow mums on her front porch, pumpkin sitting off to the side, and decorative fall wreath hanging on the front door.

Jason knew his own place could use a welcoming touch, but he'd been traveling so much since moving in at the beginning of the summer he'd barely done more than mow the lawn every so often. He'd at least met most of the neighbors, Amy included, but between long hours at work and weekends away, he'd barely gotten to know any of them.

Yet.

He wouldn't exactly mind getting up close and personal with her now that she seemed to be single again. The guy she'd been with all summer had disappeared.

Not that he minded.

Jason quietly shut the trunk of his black sports car and stole one last glance across the street. Amy's house looked warm and inviting, almost cheerful even, compared to his own. He'd barely had time to unpack all his belongings, let alone decorate.

Not that decorating was really his thing anyway, he thought with a chuckle.

He had what he needed and was fine with that.

As he reached out to open the glass storm door, he caught a glimpse of himself in his olive and khaki "Greens"—the uniform he wore to work on base every day.

The women around here didn't seem to mind the uniform, not that he'd really met any that sent his adrenaline spiking aside from his neighbor. But it sure beat the camo and gear he'd hauled around while deployed in the desert.

Four tours of duty in Afghanistan, and it felt great to be stationed stateside. Hopefully he wouldn't be required to leave the good ole U.S. of A. anytime soon, either. Constant deployments were for the younger guys without families. Not that he had anyone waiting for him in his empty house.

Not anymore.

Dropping his keys onto the table after he walked in, he headed into the kitchen. A quick appraisal of the contents of his refrigerator showed he had only milk for his cereal and a six-pack of beer. He knew that his cupboards were equally bare—he'd been gone again last weekend and hadn't made it to the store yet.

His gaze drifted to his kitchen windows and the house across the street.

He should ask her out sometime.

Make a move before some other guy swooped in and did it before him.

First things first though. After sitting at a desk all day in Quantico, he needed some fresh air. To feel the wind in his face and the solid ground beneath his feet. To let the rhythm of his movement drown out any other thoughts.

Time to get a move on.

# Chapter 2

Amy walked into her cozy living room, unceremoniously dumping her bags on the ground. The black duffle bag that landed on the hardwood floor contained her "work" clothes—jeans and a tee shirt with the name of the preschool written on it. Although they were casual, they weren't exactly something she'd go for a run in.

The tote bag landed on the bold-print area rug she'd painstakingly hunted for. Amy had been thrilled when she'd been able to purchase her own home several years earlier, and she'd spent hours searching online and in all the local stores to find the perfect furniture and accents for her space.

The walls were adorned with her own artwork—bold, modern abstracts in colorful patterns as well as a few more subdued pieces, including one of a graceful ballet dancer. The pieces were large, and took up much of the wall space, but they matched perfectly with the rest of her décor. She'd hung the drapes high above the windows, giving the room a much larger feel, and with the chic accents she'd placed throughout, Amy could almost envision that she was walking into her own personal art gallery.

*Someday,* she promised herself. *Someday.*

The spare bedroom/office/art studio was where she painted. The room had a daybed and desk as well as easels and a large storage cabinet for all of her supplies.

A sudden *thump* sent her jumping in surprise, and she looked over to see colorful construction paper and stencils in the shapes of leaves, pumpkins, and apples spilling from her overfilled tote bag.

She bent down to gather up the supplies when her cell phone began vibrating in her purse. She pulled it out to see three missed calls from her best friend, Melissa. Frowning as she swiped the screen, she quickly answered it.

"You won't believe it!" Melissa sobbed into the phone.

"What's wrong? Melissa? Are you okay?"

"He broke up with me!" Melissa shrieked hysterically.

"What?!" The papers Amy was holding slowly fluttered back to the floor. "Are you serious?"

"The wedding is two months away," Melissa continued. "TWO."

"What?" Amy repeated, still in shock.

"You heard me right—it's over."

"I can't believe it—that doesn't even make any sense. Did he say why? Maybe he just has cold feet…," Amy hedged.

"Cold feet. Right. He said he realized that he's not ready to settle down. He's thirty-two for God's sake! I mean it's not like we're college students or something. We've been together for three years. THREE years. *He* proposed to *me!*"

"What a jerk," Amy said, sinking down onto the sofa.

Melissa and Michael had seemed like the perfect couple. They had been practically inseparable when they first began dating. Michael was a Marine stationed nearby in Quantico, Virginia. He'd frequently driven up to their neighboring town to see Melissa, and although Amy knew it was hard on both of them during his year-long deployment to Afghanistan, she thought they'd been happily planning their wedding—or at least Melissa had been happily planning it.

"It's unbelievable. Un-FREAK-ing believable. I mean, I just talked to his mom the other day about floral arrangements. Floral arrangements! She had some great ideas, actually," Melissa interjected, sniffling. "But now this? After everything we've been through, it's just OVER?"

"What happened?"

"We were supposed to meet with the caterer today—to finalize the menu, go over the head count. Anyway, Michael came over to my place to pick me up. He's been working the late shift down at Quantico, so I hadn't seen him since Sunday. It's not a big deal though—I've gotten used to his crazy schedule. Anyway, as soon as he got here, I knew something was wrong. His face was all stiff and serious, his body language was off—he didn't even kiss me hello!"

"So, I take it you never made it to the caterer?"

"Nope. He gave me the whole, 'Sit down, we need

to talk,' thing."

"Let me guess. 'It's not you, it's me?'"

"Exactly. I mean, I get that it was hard when he was gone last year. I get it—I was *living* it. But he came back, we readjusted, and everything's been great. We've been planning the wedding, looking at houses, making plans for the future...."

"You're not pregnant are you?"

"Of course not!"

"All right, calm down. I just wondered if something completely freaked him out."

"Apparently the idea of marriage was enough to do that all on its own. He said he's been feeling unsure ever since he's been back."

"Wow."

"Yeah, you'd think he could have mentioned it. We could've postponed the wedding or talked about it, not acted like everything was all lovey-dovey and perfect as we planned it and continued our march to the altar."

"Maybe he didn't know," Amy said gently. "I mean, let's try to look at this in a different light. At least he didn't literally leave you at the altar. Wouldn't that have been a million times worse?"

She heard Melissa sigh on the other end of the line.

"Want to come over? I just got back from a run. I'll jump in the shower, and by the time you get here we can have leftover lasagna and a bottle of red."

"I'm not hungry."

"At least come over for a little while. I'm sure you could use a distraction right now."

"Could I ever. I've been trying to call you all afternoon."

"Sorry. I left my cell phone in the car when I was jogging."

"In the car?"

"Yeah, I went for a jog on the hiking trail."

"Well, you should bring your phone," Melissa sniffed. "What if you get attacked by a bear or something?"

"A bear?" Amy asked, trying not to smile. "In the middle of broad daylight?"

"You never know. Anyway, I wondered where you had disappeared off to." She sniffled again, and Amy was relieved that although Melissa was still upset, she wasn't sobbing as she had been when she first called. "I'll head over in a few minutes. See you in thirty?"

"Sounds perfect. See you then."

\*\*\*

"Men really suck," Melissa muttered an hour later, pouring herself a second glass of wine. She set the bottle back down on the kitchen table, which Amy had already set for dinner. "I mean first, Ben dumps you—" Melissa continued.

"Well, technically I dumped Ben; he just got over me really quickly," Amy interrupted, walking over to pull the lasagna she was reheating from the oven.

"I still don't know why you broke up with him. But he started dating that other woman like a minute later, so it was practically like he dumped you. Besides, who gets engaged to someone they just met?"

"Great, that makes me feel so much better," Amy countered, carrying the steaming hot tray over to the table. She grabbed a serving spoon and scooped them each a slice of mouth-watering lasagna. "Things were getting more serious between us, but it's not like he proposed to me. Then a few weeks after he started dating that other woman? Suddenly he's out buying wedding rings."

"Maybe they'll break up and call off the wedding. It happens I hear," she added sarcastically.

"I'm sorry, hun," Amy said.

Melissa flipped her sleek red hair back over her shoulders and sighed. With the splotches of red across her pale, porcelain skin—not to mention puffy eyes—it was quite obvious that she'd spent the afternoon crying.

Amy could tell that she was in a mood to rant and rave, not to have Amy gently disagree with everything she said, attempting to be the voice of reason. Melissa often said that Amy obviously must have the patience of a saint in order to deal with preschoolers all day long.

Melissa was a real estate agent and used to being aggressive to attract new clients and close the deal. She definitely wasn't used to being around young children, even though she'd looked forward to starting a family one day with her now ex-fiancé.

And she'd spent the last ten minutes—and first glass of wine—complaining, Amy had subtly tried to change the topic and calm her down. Not that her friend didn't have every right to be upset, but she was hoping to cheer her up even a little bit.

"Well, it should make you feel better! Ben was obviously a jackass if he got over you that quickly. Just like Michael is a complete bastard. Maybe we both dodged a bullet."

Amy picked up her own glass of wine. "I really

don't get Michael at all," she said, taking a sip of Shiraz. "Has he tried calling you? Maybe he'll come to his senses and change his mind."

"Please. He's probably out drinking with his Marine buddies tonight, picking up some new girl already—after all, he doesn't want to be tied down."

"I thought you said he worked the late shift," Amy said.

"Well, he'll be out there this weekend. The guy didn't even shed a single tear. And there I was, sitting there sobbing on my sofa like some teenager who'd just gotten dumped by her first boyfriend."

"He did really love you. He asked you to marry him! Maybe he just needs some time? Or got cold feet?"

"Pfffffft," Melissa said, expressing her distaste in that idea. "Michael had his chance. He had the girl, bought the ring, set the date…. It's over."

"So no second chances?"

"We broke up. Finito. Finished. Over."

Amy eyed the wine bottle and wondered if her friend had poured even more when she wasn't looking. She didn't blame her for needing an extra glass or two tonight.

"Anyway. I saw that hottie across the street when I was coming in," Melissa said abruptly. She let out a long whistle, and Amy laughed in surprise.

"Who? What are you talking about?"

"The Marine that lives across the street from you. I don't know his name. But I saw him jogging by when I pulled up—bulging biceps, a tattoo peeking out from underneath his sleeve, broad chest, strong legs…." She eyed Amy wickedly.

"You mean Jason? You just broke up with

someone!"

"I was just *dumped* by someone. But I didn't mean for me. I was thinking more along the lines that *you* haven't dated anyone in a while. Sex with the ex is always a mistake, but what about a fling with the hot neighbor instead?"

"Jason? He's way too old for me. And that's really weird; I've never seen him out jogging before. I go running all the time." Amy looked puzzled as she contemplated this new piece of information.

"He's what? Ten years older than us?" Amy's attention snapped back to her friend. "That is hardly *too old*. Ten years is nothing. And look at it this way—he's also got ten more years of *experience*."

"Experience?" Amy asked, somehow sensing where Melissa was going with this.

"Experience."

"Was Michael lacking in that area?"

"Of course not! Michael was amazing in bed. A-MAZE-ing! But I was thinking more for you."

Amy burst out laughing. "Great. I've been upset about Ben getting engaged all this time, and my new *lover* could very well have been just out my front door."

"Just across the street. I like your way of thinking," Melissa said with a grin, spilling some of her wine on the table as she excitedly picked up her glass again.

"I was being sarcastic! And I think it's time I cut you off," Amy said, taking the second bottle they'd opened away. She'd had two glasses compared to Melissa's…four? Five? Who was counting? "Ex-fiancé or not," she continued, "we still have to get to work in the morning."

"Oh, I don't have to be in until ten," Melissa said

carelessly.

"Lucky you. I've got a roomful of kids coming at nine—and I have to get there early and be ready for them."

"All right, whatever. I'll hang out here and watch some reality TV with you while you do your crafty stuff. That new dating show is on tonight. Maybe I should sign up."

Amy laughed as she cleared their plates away. Melissa had called her sobbing only several hours ago and was now checking out the men who lived on her street and talking about signing up for a dating show.

She knew Melissa's newfound cheerfulness was only the wine talking though—her friend would be upset again tomorrow, once the reality of her situation set in, and they'd have to deal with cancelling the wedding. Amy had just picked up her bridesmaid's dress two weeks ago and wondered if she could return it since it hadn't been altered yet.

She sighed, wondering what on earth had gotten into Michael. One thing was for certain: their upcoming girl's weekend away with friends couldn't get here soon enough.

# Chapter 3

Jason opened the front of his mailbox after he finished up his evening run, pulling out a pile of bills and one lonely sports magazine. He glanced at the football player on the cover, jumping midair to catch the ball. Although the guy was in good shape, Jason wondered how he'd fare during their early morning training runs. It was one thing to run around a field holding a football, but could this guy handle running distances in a uniform with full gear? Hauling an eighty-pound rucksack through a one-hundred-degree desert?

That was another beast entirely.

He wiped the sweat from his brow and turned to walk toward his house and grab a quick shower. His whole routine was off this week. He didn't normally jog around the neighborhood in the evening, preferring instead to train on base.

He'd seen the redhead staring at him as he'd jogged down the street earlier, returning from his run.

Was she a friend of Amy's? Although he'd just gotten a glimpse of her as he ran past, he thought it looked like her face was red from crying.

He guessed the redhead must be a friend or coworker—definitely not a sister. Whereas Amy was brunette, tanned, and toned, the redhead was pale and slightly more curvaceous.

He wondered if Amy had any family close by, if she were even from the area. Jason had grown up a military brat, traveling all over the world. His parents had retired out in California. His brother was also a Marine, currently deployed in the Middle East, and his cousin was an Army Special Forces officer. He barely knew any other lifestyle.

To serve and protect had been ingrained in him since he was a young boy. Since he, his brother, and cousin had all joined the military like his father and uncle, he knew the call to serve ran deep in their family.

Tossing his mail on the kitchen table, he downed a glass of cold water and then headed upstairs to grab a quick shower before dinner.

His cell phone buzzed with a text, and he grabbed it from his dresser to see a message from Tyler.

*Want to grab a beer? A couple of guys are meeting at the bar at 2200.*

Jason thumbed a response.

*Can't turn that down. I've got an empty fridge here.*

Tyler's response buzzed on his phone.

*I'm hoping to find a woman to go along with that beer tonight.*

Jason chuckled before heading into the bathroom. He'd been like that once, too—happy to take home a new woman every night. It didn't necessarily mean he was content to play that game anymore.

Catching a glimpse of himself in the bathroom mirror, he could see the way his biceps bulged in the white tee shirt that he was wearing, the anchor and globe of his Marine Corps tattoo just peeking out from beneath the sleeve.

He was dripping in sweat from his run, but he looked strong and healthy—his blue eyes alert, his skin still slightly tanned from time spent outdoors, his dark brown hair cropped short.

He smirked at the memory of Red watching him. Although he was used to getting attention from women, she wasn't really his type. Any woman that would stand there on the street ogling him as he jogged by wasn't someone he was interested in. That was way too obvious.

And probably the exact type of woman who'd be hanging out at the bar tonight.

He seemed to always fall for the more sweet and subtle, girl-next-door type.

The one that was a bit more of a challenge.

Nothing like making a good girl come apart in his arms, he thought with a smirk. Although he certainly wasn't one of the bad boys on base, he more than knew his way around a woman's body. Was more than adept at pleasuring a woman.

And hell if he didn't enjoy it just as much as them.

Stripping off his shirt, he turned on the shower, letting the water heat up.

His cock was already hardening as he thought of his neighbor Amy's tempting curves. Nope, Red definitely wasn't anyone he'd be chasing after. Not tonight and not ever.

But her friend Amy?

Another story altogether.

\*\*\*

Jason sauntered into the bar an hour later, nodding at some of the guys he recognized from base. Hell. One of them had a woman practically draped over him, and the other was chatting it up with two college coeds.

He was getting too damn old for this scene.

Jason walked up to the bar and ordered a beer, his eyes sweeping the room for Tyler. He took a pull from the longneck that the bartender set down in front of him and then did a double-take as the cloying scent of too much perfume suddenly assaulted his senses.

"Are you here alone, sailor?" a scantily clad woman asked as she sidled up to him.

"Little Creek's a few hours south of here," Jason said, trying not to roll his eyes as she leaned over to give him an eyeful of her ample cleavage.

Fake tits, bleached hair, and no inhibitions was so not his type.

"Little Creek?"

"It's a naval base near Virginia Beach stationed with sailors. Quantico is full of Marines."

"I see," she purred. "I could use a good, strong Marine to take me home tonight," she said suggestively, licking her lips. "Are you up to the job?"

Jason tried not to smirk. "I'm sorry, but I'm not interested."

She pouted as she walked away, and Jason shook his head in disbelief, taking another pull of his beer.

Women like that didn't care whose bed they ended up in—as long as it was a military man. That might work for the twenty-year-old kids who'd just joined the Corps, but he was long past that stage in life.

"Glad you could make it, man," Tyler said a moment later, sliding onto the empty barstool beside him, beer already in hand. His eyes followed the blonde woman Jason had just shot down.

"Ten years ago, she would've been just my type," Jason said with a chuckle.

Tyler grinned and took a swig of his beer. "Hell, if you're not interested in that pretty little thing, I might have to go introduce myself later. She was gorgeous. I sure wouldn't mind taking her home with me tonight."

"Hell. Do your thing, man. Been there, done that," Jason said with a laugh. "Got the ex-wife and kid to prove it."

Tyler guffawed. "I wish I could say I feel ya, man, but I've never been down that road."

"It was good while it lasted," Jason admitted. "I'm just not into the love 'em and leave 'em stuff anymore."

"And that's my specialty," Tyler chuckled.

"We were all there at one point," Jason said. "Hell, enjoy it while you can. It was fine once, but I've got no intention of going back down that road."

"I think I just might. Hoorah," Tyler said, standing up. He clinked his beer bottle against Jason's, and interest flashed through his eyes as he caught sight of the bleached blonde again. She waggled her fingers at him from across the bar, and Tyler glanced back at Jason. "I'm about to go get lucky. Catch you on the flip side."

Jason laughed and took a long pull from his bottle as his buddy walked away. After a hell of a long day at work, the last thing he needed was a one-night-stand with a stranger.

Especially a woman who might as well have had "easy" stamped across her forehead. Some guys were after a sure thing, but hell. There was something to be said about the thrill of the chase.

His phone buzzed in his pocket, and he pulled it out to see his ex-wife's name on the screen. With the time difference between here and the west coast, she was probably just getting off work.

"Hey. Is everything okay?" he asked in a low voice.

"Yeah, everything's fine. I just wanted to check in with you about Thanksgiving. You're still taking Brian to your parents' house, right?"

"That's the plan. Does that still work? I'll fly out to California for a few days, spend some time with him and visit my family."

"That sounds good. I don't think he remembers that you were coming then, so I just wanted to double check before I told him about it. I never know where the Marine Corps is sending you."

"You know I never had control over that," Jason said. "But I'm not deploying anywhere during this stint in Quantico."

"I understand. I just wanted to check before I told him."

"Hell. How'd he get so big anyway? Some days it feels like we just brought him home from the hospital."

Kristin laughed. "He's four going on fourteen I think. I'd put him on to say hi, but we're at soccer right now. It's the last game of the fall season. I just wanted to quick give you a call."

"Hell. Send me some pictures, all right? I wish I'd

gotten to see him play this year."

"Me too," Kristin said. "There's no chance you'll be moving out to California?"

"Not likely. I'm training some of the Marines here for the next few years. And after that? Who knows. Maybe it'll be time to leave the Corps."

"All right. We'll see you in a few weeks then."

Jason said goodbye and hung up the phone, taking another pull of his beer as he stood up. He glanced across the bar to see Tyler, his arm slung around the blonde woman from earlier. Tyler tossed some money down on the counter, and the two of them headed out of the bar together.

Jason muttered a curse.

He really was too damn old for this.

# Chapter 4

Amy glanced around her classroom the next morning, ready for the little faces that would soon come walking in through the door. When she was a kid it was always her mom who dropped her off at school, but these days moms, dads, grandparents, and even nannies were the norm.

"Hi Chelsea!" she called out to a little blonde girl walking into the classroom, holding on to her dad's hand.

"Hi Miss Amy," the little girl said shyly.

"I think she's coming down with a cold, so please give us a call if we need to come pick her up."

"Of course," Amy replied, guiding Chelsea over to a seat. "I'll keep an eye on her."

Two more kids came walking in with their parents, one crying as he clung tightly to his mother. The beginning of each class was the hardest until the kids were all seated, the parents gone, and the class had started the day's activities. Then they could ease into their routine and before she knew it, three hours would have passed by and the parents would return.

Her gaze swept around the room, making sure each child was occupied.

A moment later, her phone began vibrating on her desk, and she hurried over to turn it off. It was unlike her to forget and leave it on, but she'd been distracted this morning as she rushed off to work. Melissa had ended up spending the night, which was for the best given her state the night before. Well, that and the amount of wine that she'd consumed.

They'd had breakfast together, and Melissa had been in no hurry to leave this morning, since it turned out her first showing was pushed back until eleven-thirty. Amy had rushed around trying to get ready as Melissa lounged on the sofa, watching the morning talk shows. Then Amy's ex-boyfriend had randomly texted her, asking if he could stop by one day to pick up some skiing equipment that he'd left in her basement.

She couldn't even recall why he'd needed to store it there and wondered where he could be going skiing in November, but she hoped he'd at least come by alone.

Then as she'd been packing up her car, ready to head off to work, her neighbor Jason had called out hello to her from across the street. She'd been so startled she almost dropped the materials she was carrying for school.

Jason wasn't ever around when she left in the morning, and truth be told, she wasn't used to neighborly chats with anyone at that hour.

Especially not with the good-looking Marine who lived right across the street.

She glanced at the text from Melissa.
*Are you out of coffee?*
She rolled her eyes before stuffing her phone back into her purse.

Couldn't Melissa figure out how to open the cupboard and look for a fresh can? Honestly. And did she really expect Amy to answer her while in the midst of teaching a class full of preschoolers? Although her friend might be killing it as a realtor, she didn't have the first clue about caring for children.

She probably should've texted her ex back, too, but there was no rush for that either.

Her friend Carrie poked her head in the classroom door. "Knock, knock! How's it going?" she asked, walking over to Amy.

"Good," Amy said, eyeing the stack of papers she was carrying. "What's that?"

"For the parents," Carrie explained. "These are reminders about the bake sale next week."

"Fantastic," Amy said, taking hers from the pile. "I've got a hot date with my kitchen this weekend—pun intended."

"Ha ha. You looked ready to throttle your purse a minute ago," Carrie said with a chuckle.

"Oh, it's nothing," Amy said with a sigh. "Just too much going on at the moment to respond to everyone. My ex texted me, and a friend of mine stayed over last night because she was upset about a breakup. It's just been one thing after another today."

"I hear ya," Carrie said, eyeing the classful of kids.

"Miss Amy!" several little voices began to call out, and she said goodbye to her coworker and turned her attention back to her students as her friend moved on to the next class.

There was little else that she loved more than being in the classroom, and the kids deserved her full attention. Melissa and her ex and everyone else trying to get a hold of her this morning would just have to wait until later.

\*\*\*

Jason pulled up to the gates at Quantico, flashing his military ID. The guards glanced at his credentials and waved him through, and he drove onto base.

God, some of these kids looked young, he thought. He'd undoubtedly looked the same way when he'd joined the Marines at eighteen, but man, if it didn't make him feel old to see these fresh-faced guys around base.

He could keep up with the best of them, but while their priorities each weekend were hitting the bars with their buddies and looking for the nearest pretty girl, Jason had other responsibilities now.

And if he met the right woman someday?

He wouldn't be opposed to doing it all over again.

He flew out to California as often as he could to see Brian now that he was back stateside, but if that constant travel alongside his long work hours didn't make finding and maintaining a relationship difficult, if not damn near impossible, he wasn't sure what did. He'd barely had time to see his neighbors, let alone get out much with any of the guys on base or meet any new friends since moving here over the summer. Hopefully once the new custody arrangement was settled, he'd get to see more of Brian. He wasn't holding his breath though. Although things with Kristin were surprisingly civil, his military status and constant deployments made it easy to see why the judge had granted sole custody to her.

Now that Brian was a little older and Jason was stationed in Virginia, he was hoping they could work out a new agreement. Anything that would let him see his son more and avoid the constant cross-country flights was bound to be better for him.

He just hoped it would also be better for Brian. A boy needed his father, and he would do his damned best to make sure he was there for him. Hell, Jason's parents had been married forty years. It was hard not to want the same thing for himself now that he was older.

"Jason, wait up, man!"

He glanced behind him to see Tyler jogging down the hall to catch up with him.

"Running late this morning?" Jason asked, raising his eyebrows.

Tyler fell in step beside him as they walked down the hall toward their offices, and Jason chuckled as he saw the shit-eating grin on his face.

"I might have had something keeping me occupied. Someone, anyway."

"I take it last night went well? The blonde from the bar?"

"Fucking spectacular. She was a tiger in bed," he added with a chuckle. "I'm talking blindfolds, handcuffs, the whole nine yards."

"She have a name?" Jason asked.

"Blondie. Betty. The hell if I know. I left her naked in my bed, completely satisfied. I'm pretty sure I'll be seeing her again."

"You left her alone in your apartment?"

Tyler shrugged. "She's in her senior year of

college—no classes today. I gave her a few screaming orgasms before I left. Hope she didn't wake up the neighbors."

"She'll eventually notice if you don't know her name," Jason pointed out.

"Touché. I told her to leave her number for me. Hopefully she signs it with her name and not a kiss in red lipstick."

"Planning ahead, huh?"

"Abso-fucking-lutely. I'm headed down for a briefing. Catch up with you later, all right?"

"Have a good one."

Tyler hurried down the hall, and Jason entered his own area of offices, the scent of coffee accosting him as he chuckled.

Hell. He'd been like that once, too. Chasing after all the pretty girls at the bar. Taking one home for the night before dashing off to base in the morning.

That was a hell of a long time ago though.

"Morning, Sir," one of the young Marines said as Jason walked in, immediately snapping to attention.

His gaze swept to the lower ranking Marine. "Morning, Smith. Do you have those briefs ready for me?"

"Yes, Sir," he replied, handing Jason the thick stack of files. "They're all there. The ones you indicated were a priority are at the top."

Jason eyed the pile with disdain. "Excellent. I don't think I'll ever get used to the amount of paperwork at a desk job," he added with a chuckle. "Have you deployed much?"

"Two tours of duty in Afghanistan, Sir."

Jason nodded. "I'll be in my office. See you in the meeting at ten hundred."

"Yes, Sir, I'll be there."

"Excellent. Dismissed."

The young Marine saluted and walked away as Jason carried the files to his office. Dropping them to his desk and eyeing the huge stack, he let out a groan. He'd be reading through the materials all day. First things first though—he really needed a strong cup of coffee.

## Chapter 5

"Unbelievable," Amy muttered to herself that afternoon, heaving Ben's skiing equipment up the stairs from her basement. She nearly tripped over the gear, and grasped it more tightly so she didn't scrape the paint on her walls.

Ben wanted to stop by *with* his new girlfriend? On their way to the airport?

She didn't think so.

She'd told him she'd leave everything on the front porch. No way was she waiting around for them to come by together on their way to a romantic ski retreat.

*No way.*

She could just imagine them holed up in some ski resort in Colorado. Snuggling in front of the fire—no, *making love* in front of the fire, in the privacy of their own suite. Why bother bringing skis at all? Would they even leave their room? Ha.

As if she needed to start her weekend this way.

Friday afternoons were supposed to be relaxing. Instead of going on a run, she'd rushed home to gather his things. And now she had to *leave*. It wasn't like she was going to sit around waiting for him.

Ugh.

Amy dropped the gear on the front porch, watching as one of the ski poles clattered to the ground. She could leave it there, but then Ben would probably think she'd thrown it down on purpose.

Amy sighed as she shoved the ski pole back into the bag. She had broken up with Ben. It was her fault they weren't still together. But somewhere in the back of her mind she'd always thought they'd work things out.

She never considered that he'd move on so quickly with someone else.

That he'd be getting *married* when she hadn't had so much as a date in months.

Where would she meet someone anyway, working at a preschool?

The other teachers were all women. Most of the parents were married, and it wasn't like she planned to chase after a single dad.

Walking back inside, she hurried upstairs to change. She pulled on her black running tights, a snug tee shirt, and lightweight fleece zip-up. Pulling her hair up into a ponytail, she thought she heard a car door slam outside.

*Damn it.*

She'd been hoping she'd be long gone by the time Ben arrived. She quickly decided that she'd head out the back and cut through her neighbor's yard, jogging down the street before circling back to her own street later on. She was not in the mood for a friendly chat with Ben and certainly not in the mood for Ben plus one.

Quietly sliding open the glass door leading to her deck, she smiled as she adjusted her ponytail. Her car was in the driveway, so he knew that she was at home. He also knew she ran every afternoon, so there was no reason to stick around and make small talk.

If anyone asked, she was long gone before he even arrived, thank you very much.

Thankful that her neighbors weren't there to see her jogging through their backyard, Amy came out on the street just behind hers. It ran parallel to her own, and she'd jog down it to the main road leading toward the trails she usually ran on. She'd have to make do with a shorter workout today, but she could already begin to feel the tension leaving her body and her head beginning to clear as her feet pounded on the pavement.

After a week of teaching preschoolers and dealing with the problems of seemingly everyone else in her life, she was finally, blissfully alone.

\*\*\*

Jason squinted at the sight of someone coming toward him in the distance later that afternoon. The sun was starting to set, but as it went down, it was practically blinding him as he jogged up the street toward his neighborhood.

Still, the person running toward him almost looked like his neighbor Amy. At that moment she veered left, turning onto their street, and as he glanced away from the direction of the sun to catch sight of her profile, he was certain. He'd recognize that silky brown hair (now pulled back in a high ponytail that bounced up and down as she ran) and those luscious curves anywhere.

He felt a tightening in his groin as he realized her ponytail wasn't the only thing bouncing as she moved. Her tight tee shirt was stretched across her breasts, and although he was sure she had a sports bra or something similar, there was no doubt she was all woman underneath her running attire.

Although the rest of her body was tight and toned, those breasts could be described as nothing other than voluptuous. In a flash he imagined her wet, naked in the shower after her run. Water dripping over her, his name on her lips.

He chuffed out a laugh—he would be in need of a majorly cold shower if he kept up this line of thinking.

Swiping his forearm across his brow, he watched her jogging down their street ahead of him.

Football. A game was on later tonight. He'd think about football.

And his trip out to California next weekend. His son.

His body began to relax ever-so-slightly, and he mentally made a list of all the things he'd need to pack.

He was gaining on her as he jogged along the road, his long strides making it easy. He decided to pick up the pace.

\*\*\*

Thank God Ben's car was gone, Amy thought as she slowed her pace to jog down her own street. She knew he wouldn't stick around. After all, she'd left his things on the front porch exactly as promised.

But her leaving his things out front sent a clear message—get lost.

Her short run had cleared her head though. The crisp autumn air filled her lungs, blood pumped through her body, and she couldn't remember the last time she'd felt so alive. All in all, the weekend was now off to a great start. She had plans to kick back and relax at home tonight, but tomorrow she and Melissa were going out with a group of their girlfriends. Drinks and dinner sounded like an awesome way to catch up and spend a Saturday night.

Frowning, Amy realized that she heard footsteps pounding the pavement behind her. Footsteps that were ever so steadily getting closer.

*It was just another jogger,* she reassured herself.

She glanced back over her shoulder and was startled to see her neighbor Jason. Six-foot-two and the very definition of tall, dark, and handsome, she found herself slightly startled that she'd never noticed just *how* handsome before.

Sure, with his chiseled features, dark, shortly cropped hair and piercing blue eyes, she'd always thought he was attractive. But what drew her attention now were his broad shoulders and bulging biceps, his muscular chest that narrowed down to a slim waistline.

She felt a slight stirring inside her that she certainly hadn't felt with anyone since Ben. Jason was definitely as good looking as Melissa had said. How was it that she hadn't exactly noticed him before?

"Amy, right?" he asked, his deep voice rugged and sexy. Or maybe he was just slightly out of breath from his run. "We met over the summer."

"Yes," she replied, hoping she wouldn't sound as flustered as she felt. "And you're Jason?"

He easily caught up to her and slowed his pace to match hers. "Guilty as charged. I hope I didn't scare you coming up behind you like that. I was just finishing up my run."

"Oh, you're fine. I was concerned for a second when I heard you coming, but then I recognized you."

"I don't usually run around here. I'm on a different schedule this week, but I prefer to run on base."

"Yeah, I wondered—I've never seen you out before. I prefer the trails myself."

"Oh yeah? I'll have to check those out sometime."

They slowed down as they approached their own houses. "Yeah, it's gorgeous on the trails this time of year with the leaves changing color. Not quite as nice in the winter though." They both came to a stop and Amy stretched for a moment, turning left and right as Jason glanced over to her front porch.

"Expecting a delivery?"

"No," she said looking over to where his gaze fell. A huge cardboard box was sitting on her doormat, blocking the front door. "Unbelievable," she muttered, shaking her head.

"Something wrong?" he asked, meeting her gaze with his striking blue eyes.

"My ex must have dropped it off earlier. I left some things of his on the porch for him to pick up. Some skis. We broke up this summer. That must be my TV."

Jason looked slightly amused as she rambled on. "I'm sorry, it's not your problem. I just can't believe he'd leave a TV on my front porch. I told him just to keep it anyway. I mean how am I supposed to even move that thing?"

"I'll help you get it inside," Jason offered.

"Oh, you don't have to," Amy said, waving him off. "I'll just push it in the front door or something. Maybe take a sledgehammer to it."

Jason's lips quirked up. "That only works if you're destroying your ex's things."

"Yeah, probably so. And then I'd have to clean up the mess."

"I'll carry it in for you. Come on," he said, gesturing for her to follow him. "You probably don't want it just sitting in your foyer."

She followed him up her own driveway and couldn't help but stare at his ass as he moved. She bit her lip, trying to keep from laughing. He probably wasn't expecting to be ogled when he'd offered his assistance. But the man was certainly in shape. Broad shoulders, bulging biceps, and corded forearms. He could probably bench press that gigantic box if he wanted. As it were, he bent down and heaved the box containing her TV up in his arms as she watched, slightly dumbfounded.

"Okay, um, just hang on a sec." She turned her back to Jason and reached down into her shirt to retrieve her key from her sports bra.

*Note to self: find new place to store house key.* Like in her sock. Or a hidden rock. Or anywhere but her cleavage.

Jason smiled as she turned back around. Maybe he was too polite to say anything, but she was certain he knew she'd just been tugging her key from her shirt. Cheeks flaming, she struggled with putting the key into the lock. Now he'd think she was an idiot who couldn't even open up her front door.

Relief flooded through her as she finally turned the key and pushed the door open. At least, if nothing else, her home was clean and presentable. It wasn't like she'd been expecting to invite a hot Marine over for the afternoon. *While still wearing sweaty jogging clothes,* she thought with a cringe.

"So, where do you want this?" he asked, seeing a small flat screen TV already set up in her living room.

"Um, maybe the basement?" she said, gesturing toward the stairs. "Here, let me help you," she said, walking over to assist.

"I got it; no problem." Jason said, easily carrying the box downstairs. Her basement was finished, but aside from wall-to-wall carpeting and paint on the drywall, it was completely empty.

"Anywhere is fine. I wasn't really planning to have an extra TV down here."

"Well, someday you'll have kids."

"Kids?"

"Sure, you'll want a spare TV then. You'll watch your show; they'll watch theirs."

"Right," she said uneasily. What did he know about children? As far as she knew, he lived completely alone. Maybe he had some nieces and nephews or something.

Jason carefully set the box down against the far wall. "Is this all right?" he asked, glancing over to her as he stood. "I can move it somewhere else; I just figured this was out of the way."

"Yeah, that's perfect. I haven't decided what to do with the basement anyway, as you can tell. Thanks again for hauling it down here. I probably wouldn't have wanted to be tripping over it in the foyer every day."

"It's no trouble. It's pretty heavy, so let me know if you need help setting it up sometime. I'd be happy to move it for you again."

"Thanks, I appreciate it, but you've done more than enough as it is. I don't know how I would've gotten that thing inside."

"My pleasure. I should get going," he said, gesturing toward the stairs. "I need to grab a shower after that run."

"Right," Amy agreed. "I need to shower and change, too. I'm a mess right now."

His eyes warmed as he flashed her a grin. "You look perfect."

She laughed as she headed back up the stairs with Jason behind her. "I don't, but I appreciate the gesture."

"Your place is a lot nicer than mine," Jason said admiringly. "I could use a decorator or something," he chuckled. "I've been here for months, and it still looks like I just moved in. I love those abstract pieces. Where did you buy your artwork?"

"Oh, I actually painted those myself," Amy said, feeling a slight flush come over her. Usually everyone she had over already knew that she painted. It was actually pretty flattering to have someone that had no idea they were her own work give her a compliment like that.

"You're a painter?"

"Preschool teacher actually. But I paint in my spare time."

"Consider me impressed. These are amazing."

"Thank you," Amy replied with a genuine smile.

"Seriously, you could sell these if you wanted. They're that good."

"Maybe someday. For now, teaching it is."

Jason eyed the painting of the ballet dancer a moment longer before locking eyes with Amy. "So, I'll see you soon," Jason replied, flashing her another grin. "Just give me a holler if you have any more ex-boyfriends leaving TVs or other large stereo equipment at your front door."

"Right," she said, blushing again. What was it about him that got under her skin? He was just teasing her for heaven's sake. "See you soon."

Jason turned and pulled open the door, sauntering down her driveway without so much as a backward glance. *He didn't mean anything by that*, Amy told herself as she closed the door behind him.

They were neighbors.

Of course she'd see him again. Soon.

She smiled and practically bounced into the kitchen to grab a glass of water before her shower. Why did it suddenly feel like her day had ended on a much better note than it had started with?

# Chapter 6

"So he came over *with* his new girlfriend?" Amy's friend Beth asked the next evening.

The girls were out at a local restaurant and bar, waiting for Melissa and their friend Kara to arrive. Melissa had already texted them to say that she'd be running late. She'd spent the afternoon with Michael, presumably sorting through all that needed to be cancelled for the wedding that would never be.

Amy was certain that Melissa would be heaping mad by the time she arrived, and this was probably her only chance to vent to Beth about her own ex.

Their friend Kara was married and the mother of twin baby girls. It was a given that she'd be late on the rare occasion that she joined the rest of them for dinner or drinks.

"Yep," Amy replied. She took a swig of her beer and glanced around the crowded bar area. It wasn't likely that she'd see any of her students' parents while out, but she tried to be careful when in public. Not that she was really one to go wild anyway. *That was more Melissa's forte*, she thought with a smirk.

"What's so funny?" Beth asked, catching her expression.

"Oh, it's nothing."

"So what'd you say?"

"To who?"

"Ben," Beth said, looking a little frustrated.

"Oh, when he came over? I didn't say a thing. I snuck out the back door."

Beth choked on the margarita she was sipping. "You're kidding! Did he know you were there?"

"Nope," Amy said with a grin. "I left his things on the front porch for him to pick up."

"What'd you do out back?"

"I went for a run," Amy recalled with a laugh. "I cut across the neighbor's yard and headed out to the main road before eventually looping back. I was feeling pretty good, too. Then I ran into my neighbor, who was also out jogging. Melissa has the hots for him," she added confidentially.

"Melissa? But Michael just broke up with her like two seconds ago!"

"Oh, I know. I'm just teasing. She saw him the other day when she came over and was going on and on about how gorgeous he was."

"So you ran away from your ex to go jogging with another man instead."

"Well, we didn't really run together. We ran into each other and jogged by about five houses as we returned to our own. Oh, and get this…." Amy proceeded to tell her about the TV on her front porch and Jason carrying it inside.

"That's really weird. Why would he bring over

your TV if he was on his way to the airport?"

Amy shrugged. "Who knows. Maybe his new girlfriend wanted it gone or something. His fiancée, I should say. I probably would have left it right there on the porch if Jason wasn't around."

"God, too bad he didn't show up when you and Jason were jogging down the street together."

"Yeah, that would've been ideal, wouldn't it? Letting him think I've moved onward and upward?"

Beth chuckled. "Men always want what they can't have. He'd probably propose to you, too, if he saw that."

Amy snorted, nearly spitting out her beer. "Trust me, we're not getting back together."

"Well, like you said. Onward and upward." She raised her margarita, and Amy clinked her beer bottle against the glass as she laughed.

"I'll drink to that," she said, taking a pull of her beer.

They'd moved on to other topics and their second drink each by the time Kara and eventually Melissa arrived. Kara looked completely frazzled after leaving her husband home with their twins, and Melissa, as predicted, looked furious.

"Aaaaand we're through," Melissa announced twenty minutes later, slamming her shot glass down on the counter. She'd insisted on ordering them all a round of shots before telling them about her afternoon with Michael. Only Beth had joined her as Kara was still breastfeeding and Amy didn't do shots.

"You really don't want yours?" Melissa asked Amy, fingers winding round the glass.

"Have at it."

Melissa downed it in one gulp. "Ah, I really needed

that this afternoon. What a massive headache I have from even attempting to have a conversation with that man."

"So it's definitely over?" Kara asked, attempting to be the voice of reason. "Are you sure he won't have a change of heart?"

"Absolutely. Michael offered to reimburse me for some of the wedding costs I'd paid for. I mean, my God, it's the LEAST he could do. The very LEAST. Who calls off their wedding with only two months to go? I am over men. OVER them. And if I see that bastard out here tonight with another woman, I swear I will—"

"Shhh, calm down!" Amy chastised.

"Trust me," Melissa said, rolling her eyes. "If the same thing happened to any of you, you would be pissed off as well."

"Touché," Beth said

"So he wasn't sorry at all?" Amy asked, looking doubtful. "You guys were together for three years—you'd think he'd have some regrets."

"He was sorry he came over, that's for sure."

The girls all laughed. Melissa was known for her melodrama, but there was no doubt that she would have given Michael hell now that she'd had a few days to stew over their cancelled wedding. What had been a sob-fest at Amy's house a few days ago was no doubt a shit storm today, Amy thought with a smirk. She imagined the burly Marine quaking in his boots at Melissa's wrath. Ha.

As the wedding day drew closer, Melissa was no doubt going to be feeling upset all over again though. They were probably all going to be in for a long couple of months.

"You know, you never texted me back yesterday," Melissa suddenly recalled, glancing over at Amy.

"When did you text me?" Amy asked, confused.

"Yesterday morning, when I was desperately in search of coffee."

"They sell that stuff at the grocery stores now," Beth commented dryly.

"Ha ha, very funny," Melissa muttered. "This was more like a coffee emergency."

"I have plenty of those," Kara chimed in. "I'm running on no sleep."

"Well, you have twin babies and can hardly ever leave the house. Melissa is a grown woman perfectly capable of driving to the store. Or the nearest Starbucks."

"She was at my house," Amy explained. "Apparently opening the cupboard to search for coffee was out of the question."

"Look, I was in the middle of a crisis," Melissa said. "And maybe just a touch hung over."

"A touch," Amy commented with a laugh. "I was in the middle of a room full of preschoolers. Plus, Ben had been texting me about his damn ski equipment, so I had other things on my mind."

"She was busy planning a rendezvous with her hot neighbor," Beth added with a grin.

"What?!" Melissa shrieked, suddenly looking happier than she'd been all evening. "You went out with your neighbor? Details, please!"

"I didn't go out with him," Amy said, rolling her eyes. "I ran into him while out jogging. Or actually, he kind of chased me down the street," she said thoughtfully.

"You left out that part earlier," Beth said, raising

her eyebrows.

"Well, I certainly didn't plan to see him. But Ben had helpfully left a gigantic TV in front of my front door, so Jason offered to haul it inside for me. And yes, he is incredibly hot, but I've sworn off men for a while."

"As you should," Beth said, rolling her eyes. "You dated a guy for a couple of months and broke up. Time to become a crazy cat lady and never date again."

"You're one to talk," Amy said. "You're extremely happy with your man. And Kara is married with cute babies. I'm doing just fine on my own, thank you very much."

"Amen to that," Melissa agreed. "Men? Who needs 'em!" She gestured to the bartender to bring them another round.

\*\*\*

Jason walked out of the restaurant that night, a bag full of carry-out food gripped in his hand. The intoxicating aroma of a freshly grilled burger and fries hit him, and his stomach rumbled.

There was nothing like seeing all the fun-loving groups of friends and happy couples inside to remind him he was very much alone. He'd been gone so much since he'd moved to Virginia, what did he expect?

He had his buddies from base. His friends stationed around the globe.

Hell.

You knew you were getting old when you wished you were home with your wife and kid on Saturday night, not picking up carry-out alone. Not that he and Kristin had been happily spending Saturday nights together in a long, long time. The constant deployments made sure to kill any real shot their relationship ever had. But even a night in with his son would be a million times better than spending the weekend alone.

He clicked the remote to his sports car and was just opening the door when he did a double take as a woman across the parking lot caught his eye.

And not just any woman.

Amy.

She was wearing tight jeans, those knee-high leather boots all the women seemed to have nowadays, and a long red sweater. He wasn't sure what it was—maybe the loose way her hair cascaded over her shoulders, or the way those jeans made her legs look a mile long—but the overall look was sexy as hell.

She searched through her purse, standing right beside her SUV. His gaze swept the lot around her, but it didn't seem like she was with anyone. He watched as she flipped her brown hair back off her face. He assumed she must be looking for her keys—why else would she be standing there alone in the parking lot at this time of night?

Setting his bag of food down on the floor, Jason shut his car door and clicked the remote once again to lock it. By the time he had walked across the lot, she was stepping back from the SUV as her eyes scanned the ground.

"Amy."

She looked up, surprised, a slightly distracted look on her face. Her cheeks were a little flushed from the cool night air, but her sapphire blue eyes sparkled in the moonlight.

"Jason, hi." She glanced toward the ground again and then back at him. "I was just trying to find my keys. I swear I had them a second ago."

"Need some help?"

"Yes," she said gratefully. "I just had dinner with some friends, and they all left. Would you believe *all* of them parked in the other lot?"

He watched her rosy lips as she spoke, imagining what it might be like to kiss them someday. Would she taste as sweet as she smelled? Whatever perfume she had on right now was simply intoxicating. He'd lean closer to take a whiff if that wouldn't have been entirely inappropriate. As it were, she shivered in the cool night air, and he felt like a jerk for just letting her stand there. "Here, take my jacket," he said, shrugging out of the brown leather one that he was wearing.

"Oh, no, I couldn't. You'll be cold."

"I'll be fine. And you look like you're cold right now. I insist."

Amy hesitantly took it from him and put it on. "Well, if you're sure. Thank you."

Amy did look happier now that she was warm, even if she was still locked out of her vehicle. Not to mention pretty damn cute wearing his leather jacket. It engulfed her, covering her feminine shape, but somehow the contrast made her look that much more attractive.

They both stepped farther out from her SUV at exactly the same time, accidentally bumping into one another.

"I'm sorry," Amy said, colliding into his chest. He reached out to steady her, and she flushed as she met his gaze. Jason had to resist the urge to pull her closer. She was the perfect height for him, her head just beneath his chin. It would be so easy to bend down right now for a kiss—not that he'd be doing that here in the parking lot when he was supposed to be helping her look for her keys.

Hell, it's not like they even knew each other.

Not really.

The attraction between them felt almost palpable though, with her gaze locked with his, and the two of them standing mere inches away from one another. He worked to keep his face neutral, wondering if the heat in his eyes might give him away.

"It was my fault," he disagreed, feeling somewhat chagrined now that she was backing away. Damn if she wasn't cute though, all flustered yet sexy and feminine at the same time.

"Maybe I left them inside," she said, seeming uncertain as to what to do next.

"Let's go check. If they're not out here, I'm sure someone already found them and turned them in. But I'm happy to give you a lift home if you need it."

"Okay, thanks. I'd really appreciate it," she said, looking slightly relieved.

Had she really thought he'd just leave her stranded here alone in the parking lot late at night? Man, he'd have to work harder at being a friendlier neighbor if that's how little she thought of him. Then again, her own friends had left—not knowing she was locked out, of course. But that would leave a person feeling rattled. And they didn't know each other that well— maybe she'd thought he'd just continue on his way and let her figure it out on her own.

"Come on," he said, gesturing toward the front of

the restaurant. "Let's go check for those keys."

He rested his hand lightly on the small of her back, guiding her forward.

That was something that felt damn right about escorting her back inside. Which was crazy. She wasn't his girlfriend, much less even his date for the night.

He felt protective of her though.

Not to mention incredibly attracted to her.

He barely even knew the woman but liked everything he'd found out so far. She loved to run. She painted. She obviously loved kids.

And hell.

It didn't hurt that she was gorgeous.

He'd love to take the time to get to know her better. Ask her out. Kiss her goodnight.

It wasn't exactly the right time to ask her out now though when she was flustered and locked out of her SUV.

Something about her stirred his protective instincts though, and he wanted her to feel safe and secure when she was with him. Content that he would handle things. Drive her home, sort out a way to get her a new set of keys if she couldn't find hers.

Jason reached out to open the door to the restaurant and caught another whiff of her scent. He resisted the urge to groan. That floral perfume she had on was nearly killing him.

\*\*\*

Amy blew out a sigh as the hostess took down her name and phone number.

"We'll call you if anyone turns in a set of keys," the

hostess assured her. "Things like this happen all the time—people lose cell phones, keys, wallets. You name it. You'd be surprised by what people come in looking for sometimes," she added with a laugh.

"Okay, thank you," Amy said, her heart pounding in her chest. It was silly to be worked up over something so trivial. She had a spare key to her car at home somewhere. Jason had offered her a ride. She'd catch a cab back to the restaurant to pick up her car once she found the spare key. No big deal.

"Are you okay?" Jason asked, eyeing her as they turned away.

"Oh, yeah. I'm fine," releasing a breath. "Just flustered I guess. Nothing like standing around the parking lot in the dark realizing you have no way to leave."

"I'll give you a lift," Jason reassured her. "I'm sure your keys will turn up. And no worries, you're right on the way," he added with a wink.

Amy laughed despite herself. "Good timing on your part I suppose. My friends would've come back if I called them, but wow. What an ordeal."

"Do you have your house keys?"

"Nope," Amy said as Jason pulled open the passenger side door for her. "They were on the same keychain." He waited until she was snugly seated before closing the door, and she pulled on her seatbelt as he climbed in.

"Oh, you were picking up food!" she said with a frown as she spotted the forgotten bag on the floor of the car. "I'm sorry—it's totally cold by now."

"It's no problem," Jason said as he climbed in the driver's seat. "That's what they invented microwave ovens for."

She laughed and enjoyed the brief flash of a smile that he gave her before starting the engine. His blue eyes were sparkling, alert. Amy wondered what he was so happy about. Maybe he had a hot date later on tonight or something. *Yeah right.* It was already nine. And she'd never seen him with anyone before, come to think of it. "Well, I am sorry for messing up your dinner. But thanks again for the ride."

"Do you want me to call a locksmith?" he asked, his voice deep. "I'm not sure how long they'd take to get here on a Saturday night. Of course, you're welcome to wait over at my place until they arrive."

"I think my next-door neighbor still has a spare key. I hope so at least. I can't imagine what a locksmith would charge at this hour."

"You've got some great neighbors, huh?" Jason asked, a hint of humor in his voice. He didn't look over at her, but Amy thought she detected the hint of a smile in his profile as he stared ahead while driving.

"Pretty much," Amy replied with a laugh. "They drive me around, haul TVs inside my house for me. You know—all the usual neighborly stuff. Comes with the territory."

"The usual stuff, huh? So, I guess I fit right in."

"Well, I don't know if I could've relied on Mrs. Jones for all that heavy lifting," Amy replied, referring to the elderly widow that lived next door to her.

"Is that the sweet little old lady that bakes pies all the time?"

"The very one," Amy said with a smile. Although Jason hadn't been around much, he had made a brief appearance at the annual end-of-summer neighborhood block party. She'd been with Ben then, spending the evening drinking beers and snuggled under his arm. They'd made love on her deck under the stars that night—under the town fireworks, as well. Although they'd been much too busy creating their own fireworks to pay much attention to the town's festivities.

"She made a killer blackberry pie for that barbeque. Man—that made me miss my mom's cooking."

"Where are you from?"

"All over the place—military brat. My parents are out in California. So is the rest of my family, actually."

"Ah, a west-coast guy. I'm from Maryland, just outside of DC."

"Is your family still there?"

"My parents yes, my sister no. It's nice having them relatively close by. I can drive home in a few hours."

Jason drove down the main road she'd jogged along yesterday afternoon and swung a left back into their neighborhood. The cozy houses were warmly lit up in the cool night, and Amy felt a sudden pang of sadness that she was returning to her darkened house alone. It had been a while since a man had driven her home, she realized. She hadn't dated anyone since Ben, and he'd practically lived at her place anyway.

Now she'd had a fun evening with her girlfriends and a surprisingly enjoyable time with Jason, despite the fact that they were searching for her missing keys. It was almost a little disappointing to be spending the rest of the evening alone.

Amy hoped her neighbor Mrs. Jones would actually be home and awake at this hour. It was unlikely she'd be out unless she was gone for real—as in out of town. Bed was a different possibility though.

Amy hated to wake her if unnecessary, but what choice did she have? A locksmith would probably charge an arm and a leg on a Saturday night.

As Jason pulled into her driveway, she was relieved to see the kitchen light on at Mrs. Jones's house. She also realized that Jason had parked in *her* driveway, not his own, even though she could easily have just walked across the street from his house.

"I'll wait here," Jason said, leaning against the driver side door after they'd both gotten out of the car.

"Okay, back in a sec!" Amy jogged across the yard to her neighbor's house to ring the doorbell. Mrs. Jones opened the door wearing her robe and nightgown. She seemed surprised to see Amy and immediately asked what was wrong. After Amy explained that she needed her spare key, the woman went to retrieve it and returned a moment later. She glanced across the yard at Jason and his car in the driveway, and then handed the key to Amy with a smile.

"I won't keep you two young people. He's such a nice boy."

Amy laughed and realized she was starting to flush slightly at the woman's knowing gaze. "Oh, no. He just gave me a ride home. I lost my keys at a restaurant tonight when I was out with some girlfriends."

"All right, dear. Well you have a nice evening anyway."

"Thanks again Mrs. Jones. Goodnight!"

"Bye, dear," she said sweetly.

Amy turned and hurried back over to Jason. Only then did she realize she was still wearing his leather jacket. No wonder the older woman was suspecting that the two of them were together. "Got it," she said, holding the spare key up for him to see.

"Do you want to get your extra car key? I'll drive you back to the restaurant to pick up your car so it's not sitting in the lot all night."

"I'm afraid I need to hunt for it," she said sheepishly. "I'm not exactly sure where it is."

Jason chuckled. "All right, well tomorrow then. Or later on tonight, if you find it. I'll be up for a while, so let me know if you need a lift."

Amy nodded. "Thanks again for your help. I'd probably still be stranded out in the parking lot if it weren't for you." She shrugged out of his jacket and handed it back to him.

"It was my pleasure," Jason replied, carefully taking it back from her. She wondered the reason for his unhurried movements and realized that he seemed to be studying her features in the moonlight.

"Well, goodnight," she finally said, turning to go.

"Have a good night, ma'am," he replied.

"Ma'am?" she asked in surprise, glancing back before she started to walk away. "Well now I feel old."

"Honey, if there's one thing you're not, it's old," he replied in a low voice. He had that certain gleam in his eye again, and Amy wondered if she was somehow misreading him. He was so polite and careful not to accidentally touch her or overstep any boundaries, but every once in a while, he'd gotten that smoldering look in his eyes tonight.

Had he looked at her like that all summer long and she'd never even noticed? Had they ever really spent any time alone for her to even find out? Aside from the past couple of days, she hadn't really had a single significant conversation with him.

Jason was still standing at his car when she reached her front door, and she turned back to give him a small wave goodbye. He gave her a small nod as if to say, *yep, everything you're thinking is true.*

Or maybe that last part was just her imagination and he was simply saying goodnight.

# Chapter 7

The next morning, Amy's phone buzzed as she was pulling on her running clothes. She glanced at her alarm clock, frowning as she realized it was only eight thirty. She grabbed her phone from where it lay charging, and Beth's name flashed across the screen.

"Hey Beth, is everything okay?" she asked.

"Hey—I'm so sorry, but I've got your keys."

"My keys?! I spent an hour looking for them last night at the restaurant. Where were they?"

"I'm sorry—I must have picked them up off the table or something as we were getting ready to leave. I didn't even realize that I had them until this morning. They were in my coat pocket of all places. I'll bring them by in a little while. How did you get home? Did Melissa or Kara give you a ride?"

"No, you guys had all left when I realized I lost my keys. I ran into my neighbor in the parking lot, and he gave me a ride—"

"Major McHottie?"

"Major McWhattie?" Amy asked with a laugh. "I have no idea what rank he is, but if you're referring to Jason, then yes, that's who. Luckily, he spotted me, or I would've needed to call one of you to come back and drive me home. He was picking up food and happened to see me there alone in the parking lot. My next-door neighbor had a spare key to my house, but Jason had to give me a ride."

"Well that doesn't sound *so* bad. Stranded in the parking lot with a hot Marine rushing to your rescue?"

Amy snorted. "Right. With me flustered and distracted."

"Well, maybe he has a thing for damsels in distress."

Amy crossed her bedroom to grab her running shoes from her closet. "Maybe, maybe not. It doesn't matter either way since he's my neighbor. Plus the fact that I'm not interested in dating anyone right now."

"Um-hmm," Beth said smugly. "That's what they all say. How about I pick you up in a little while? I'll treat you to brunch, and then we can swing by the restaurant to get your car."

"Sounds perfect. I was just getting ready to head out on a run though. Want to come by in an hour? Or are you ready to eat now?"

"An hour from now sounds perfect. And don't forget, brunch is on me."

"Well, it's the least you can do," Amy teased. "Especially after a hot Marine had to come to my rescue after you abandoned me."

Beth snorted. "Told you so."

Amy laughed as she sank down onto her bed,

shoes in hand. "I better get going if I want to get a run in before brunch. See you soon!"

They said goodbye, and she set her phone down on the nightstand.

Good grief.

All her worry last night had been for nothing. At least her keys had been found. Hopefully her car would be okay after leaving it in the parking lot all night. She blew out a sigh.

First things first—a run to get her blood pumping, and then brunch with one of her best friends.

Not a bad way to start a Sunday.

\*\*\*

An hour later, the girls were happily ensconced in a cozy booth at the local diner. Amy took a careful sip of her steaming hot coffee, laughing as Beth continued to tell her about the night before.

"I mean seriously, I could not get the guy to turn off the TV," Beth continued, complaining about her boyfriend. "I get that we live together, but seriously? I had to put on some lingerie and prance around in front of him to get the guy to come to bed."

"You pranced around? I seriously doubt that."

"All right, so I concede that there was no actual prancing involved. It sure felt like it though."

Amy raised her eyebrows, looking doubtfully at her friend.

"There was lingerie. Black lace."

"We should all have your problems. A gorgeous boyfriend who lives with you, a kickass lawyer job where you make the big bucks, a sweet condo that's like a million square feet—"

"You have a house!" Beth said, looking at Amy in disbelief. "And I know you're upset about Ben getting engaged so quickly—I get it. But *you* broke up with *him*. There had to be a reason behind that other than just being scared, am I right? He obviously wasn't the guy for you."

"No, I guess he wasn't," Amy agreed.

"That's it?" Beth asked, raising her eyebrows. "No argument from you, no pining for the one who got away?"

Amy laughed and took another sip of her coffee. "Was I really that bad?"

"Of course not. Not nearly as bad as Melissa is going to be. I just expected a little more of the 'I miss Ben' talk. And the lawyer in me wanted to argue about why he's all wrong for you."

"No more Ben talk. That train has passed."

"I'm holding you to that," Beth said with a grin. "So. Kara is married, I've got Nick. Now we just need to get you and Melissa fixed up."

"No, no, no," Amy quickly disagreed. "I've completely sworn off men for a while, which you already know. And Melissa does not need a rebound guy at the moment. I'm all about work, painting, and friends right now. And of course our upcoming girl's trip."

"Oh, about that...," Beth said, sounding hesitant.

"Oh no, not you, too," Amy groaned.

"Kara told you?"

"Yes! She's not ready to leave the babies. And I totally get that. But I thought the rest of us could still hang out and have a fun weekend getaway."

"I'm sorry. I really, really want to go. And a trip right before Thanksgiving sounds amazing. But now that Nick and I are living together, I can't just leave him the weekend before our first Thanksgiving. We want to go shopping together, pick out the food, start buying Christmas decorations…. Sappy, I know. And our tickets to the spa are refundable. Remember I insisted we get that travel insurance? Plus, it was supposed to be a last girl's trip before Melissa's big day, and now she's kind of down about it with the wedding being called off…."

"Yeah, I get it," Amy said with a sigh. "I was just looking forward to a weekend away. I can't go home for Thanksgiving this year—my parents are taking that month-long cruise around Europe, my sister has a million things to do for her residency…."

Amy trailed off, thinking that for once the rest of her family had more hectic lives than she did. In the past, they'd practically been scheduling family events around her. She'd always had to stay on a stricter schedule that followed the school calendar. And this was the first year that she'd be *alone* alone, without a boyfriend.

First there was her college boyfriend. Then that rugged guy Hunter that she'd only briefly dated, but *yum*. He was rebound all the way. She'd dated her next serious boyfriend for a couple of years before ending up with Ben.

And that had crashed and burned only months after it started.

"Let's have Thanksgiving together," Beth suggested. "We'll do it at my place. *Our* place," she quickly corrected, referring to Nick. "And after the Thanksgiving stuff, we'll do a girl's day out on Friday or something. We could grab lunch and shop 'til we drop," she said, her eyes brightening as she began to organize a new plan. "For Christmas."

"That would be fun," Amy mused, remembering their earlier years of marathon shopping sessions during the holidays. Times had changed as they'd gotten older and been busy with work, boyfriends, and other commitments. But if they couldn't get away for a girl's weekend, there was certainly no reason they couldn't all spend Thanksgiving together.

"So it's okay if I text Melissa and tell her we're cancelling the girl's trip?" Beth hedged.

"I guess so," Amy said with a shrug. "When were you guys talking about it anyway? No one said anything last night."

"Oh, right after we left. Remember how we parked around back? Kara pulled me aside to ask what I thought. Melissa overheard us…."

Amy laughed. "And the rest is history. It sounds like there was no reason to talk to me then if everyone else was already out. Thanksgiving will be fun though."

"Definitely. I'll let the others know the trip is off. And invite them over for Thanksgiving."

They finished up their breakfast, and Beth drove Amy back to get her car at the restaurant. Thankfully it hadn't been towed, but she'd told the restaurant manager last night that she'd lost her keys and couldn't drive it home. She probably wasn't the first one to leave her car here—surely others either had too much to drink or hadn't gone home alone. Her SUV was the lone vehicle sitting in the lot this morning though.

The girls said their goodbyes, and Amy climbed into her SUV, pulling out onto the road. She still had cookies and apple pies to bake for the school bake sale tomorrow, not to mention countless little projects to finish for her preschool classes.

She was slightly saddened to realize she wouldn't have any time to paint this weekend. That seemed to always fall on the back burner these days, but if her choice was between dinner out with her friends last night or staying in alone to get lost in her artwork, she was happy to trade in free time at home for some much-needed time with her girlfriends. There was always winter vacation to get back into her painting.

Pulling into the lot of the grocery store, she circled around the busy lot until she found a spot in the back. Shivering slightly in the cold, she retrieved a shopping cart from the array in front of the store and pushed it inside.

Amy grabbed a few basics and then headed over to the baking aisle. Selecting a couple bags of flour, sugar, brown sugar, and chocolate chips, she quickly filled up her cart. Consulting her list, she grabbed a few more items before making her way to the checkout line.

A long line of shoppers was already in front of her, evidently starting their Thanksgiving shopping early. As she finally moved forward and began unloading everything onto the conveyor belt, a low, masculine voice beside her suddenly caught her attention. "You're not opening a bakery, are you?"

Amy turned, flushing in surprise as she saw Jason standing there. He had on dark gray sweatpants and a black Marine Corps tee shirt that nicely hugged his muscular frame. The short sleeves revealed the hint of a tattoo peeking out from beneath his left sleeve, and Amy was a little surprised. He hadn't seemed like the tattoo type of guy from what she had seen before. She imagined guys covered in tattoos to be rough, rocker types, not clean-cut military men.

What did she know anyway, though?

Lots of men in the military had tattoos.

Besides, it was just one; it's not like his whole arm was covered in ink. Amy guessed he must be on his way to the gym or something—he certainly wasn't just coming from it as she detected the clean scent of soap and aftershave as he leaned closer to inspect the contents of her cart.

"Right, in all my spare time. Preschool bake sale," she explained with a smile.

"So it's safe to assume you got your car back? Unless you're planning to wheel all this home in your shopping cart." Jason grinned down at her, his blue eyes gleaming.

"My friend Beth had my keys in her pocket! She called me this morning. Unbelievable, right? I think she accidentally grabbed them off the table when we were leaving the restaurant."

"That's crazy. I'm glad you found them—or glad she found them. Those things are expensive if you ever need to have a new one made."

"It would've been nice if she found them last night. Oh well," she added with a shrug. "At least I've got my car back now."

"True. Well, let me know if you need a taste-tester for all your baking. I'm going to go lift for a while, but I'm sure I'll work up an appetite."

He stepped slightly closer as another shopper brushed past him, and she resisted the urge to move away. Jason was so close, she could feel the heat radiating off him. And she enjoyed the closeness a little more than she wanted to admit.

"I'll keep you in mind," she teased.

"Fantastic. I'm going to hit the express lane," he said, glancing back at the line behind her.

Her gaze fell to the pack of protein bars in his hand.

"That's it?" she asked with a laugh.

"I'm a simple guy," he said, the corner of his mouth quirking up in a smile as he backed away. "I'll see you later."

Amy waved goodbye, feeling a flush spread over her cheeks, and finished loading her groceries onto the belt.

It was strange that Jason was never usually around on the weekends, yet she'd seen him several times over the past few days. Had they been crossing paths before and she'd just never known it?

She finished checking out and pushed her cart outside, her eyes sweeping around the parking lot. Of course he was already gone. She had an entire cart full of food compared to his one lone purchase.

And she didn't really need to see him again anyway.

He lived across the street for heaven's sake.

The memory of those blue eyes gazing down at her and his large frame standing over her sent warmth coursing through her entire body though.

For her being intent on not dating anyone right now, Jason was on her mind an awful lot of the time.

## Chapter 8

Jason paused in the middle of hammering his bookshelf together, listening again for what had sounded like the doorbell. Deciding he could use a break anyway, he walked downstairs and was surprised to see a plate of cookies sitting on his front porch. A smile came to his face as he realized that they were from Amy. There was no note—she'd probably assumed she'd find him at home since his car was in the driveway.

Carrying the plate into the kitchen, he popped one into his mouth. Damn they were delicious. And still warm. He polished it off before walking back to the front door.

Jogging across the street, he rang the doorbell at Amy's house, wondering if he was interrupting her baking session. A blast of warm air and the scent of cookies greeted him as she opened the front door. Her welcoming little home was a far cry from his own. He'd been there for months and was still assembling his furniture.

Amy appeared from behind the front door, wearing jeans and a hot pink tee shirt. Her hair was pulled back into a ponytail, her cheeks flushed, and her lips a luscious, rosy shade.

"Hi," she said brightly, a smile coming to her face at the sight of him.

"Sorry I missed you earlier. I was upstairs putting together some furniture. I just wanted to say thank you for the cookies."

"You're welcome. Thank *you* for coming to my rescue last night."

"Any time," he said with a grin. He'd just noticed that she had a smudge of flour across one cheek. He reached out, gently brushing it off with his thumb, and watched as a flush came to her face. "You had a little flour there," he said, his voice gravel.

What was it about this woman that had his mind spinning in circles, anyway?

Women pranced around in far less than she had on, but something about her overall appearance was always sexy as hell.

"Oh," she said, blushing even more. "I didn't even glance in the mirror before I ran to the door. My kitchen is a disaster right now."

"Well, I don't want to intrude. I just thought I'd run over and thank you in person while I had a chance."

"Yeah, I've still got more baking to do. Apple pies are up next. And after all the cookies I sampled earlier, I think I'll need to do a lot more running after the bake sale tomorrow," she added with a laugh.

Jason glanced down at her slender frame with an amused smile. She certainly looked amazing to him, but if experience had taught him anything, it was that complimenting a woman you barely knew about her looks didn't usually go over that well. Not the type of women that he seemed to like anyway. Amy's friend Red probably wouldn't have a problem with anyone lavishing her with compliments—whether she knew them or not.

He raised his eyes back up, perhaps letting them linger a moment too long on her firm, full breasts, but quickly met her eyes once more.

Amy hadn't seemed to notice, and if she did, wasn't letting on. "You've been around a lot this weekend," she commented. "I don't usually run into you."

"I travel a lot on the weekends," he explained. He didn't add that he was often going to see his young son. He knew Amy loved children, being a preschool teacher, but it seemed too soon to overcomplicate things by bringing up Brian and his ex-wife right now. "I'm hoping to change that in the future, though."

"Oh, okay," she said, seeming unsure what exactly he meant. *And rightfully so,* he thought. It wasn't like him to be purposefully vague.

Jason caught a glimpse of one of Amy's paintings on the wall, and inspiration suddenly struck. He'd ask her for help buying some artwork. God knew his place needed it. If he were ever going to gain partial custody of Brian, he needed to decorate his house—make it the least bit more lived-in and homey looking. Plus, Brian would need a room. Hell, if he were ever even going to have company over he needed to decorate a little bit.

"I noticed an art gallery in town. What do you think about going with me sometime to pick out some artwork? My walls are totally bare, and I could use some help."

"Oh, uh, sure," she said, sounding surprised.

"It's fine if you don't have the time," he reassured her. "I just love the things you painted and thought you might like to help me pick something out."

"You just caught me off guard," she said, her cheeks turning slightly pink. His eyes trailed down to her lips. "Sure, I'd love to help you. When do you have in mind?"

"How about one night after work this week?"

He'd get to know Amy a little better, she'd be at ease helping him find the perfect painting for his home, and if that went well, then he'd suggest dinner or drinks another time. A real date. It was tricky with the holidays coming up. He'd be gone a couple of weekends and then again at Thanksgiving. He really wanted to see more of her though.

"Tuesday or Wednesday would be great. The art gallery always displays beautiful pieces from local artists. Of course, the larger stores have mass-produced artwork, if you want something like that instead."

"I think the art gallery would be perfect. I wouldn't mind a custom piece or two."

"Great. Why don't I give you my cell number, and we can set up a time?"

"Sounds perfect." He palmed his pockets. "I didn't bring my phone when I ran over. I'll give you my number, and you can text me so I have yours."

"Okay, hang on," she said with a laugh. "Come in," she added, walking into her kitchen.

The snug jeans she was wearing hugged her toned ass, and he tried to stifle a groan. She had no damn idea how tempting she was.

A moment later she was back carrying her phone. He gave her his number, and she texted him right away.

"I'll be in touch," he said with a grin. "Guess I'll let you get back to it. Thanks again for the cookies."

"Sure thing," she said, walking with him toward the front door. She flushed slightly as he turned around, only inches away from her. He tried to ignore the swell of her breasts as she took a breath, or the way her eyes widened ever-so-slightly as she gazed up at him.

"I'll talk to you soon," he said in a low voice. "Bye Amy."

"Bye," she repeated softly, closing the door behind him.

He glanced back at the door as he walked down the driveway, but she was already gone. No matter. He was looking forward to the work week more than he had in a long time.

# Chapter 9

Wednesday after work, Amy got ready to meet Jason at the art gallery. They'd planned to drive over together, but he'd gotten stuck in bad traffic heading home from Quantico, and since she was working late finishing up some Thanksgiving projects for school, it had been easier to just arrange to meet him.

Amy had barely had time to change as she left the classroom. She'd switched out her school tee shirt for a fluttery, trendy blouse. Her casual shoes got swapped out for a pair of heeled boots. Glancing in the mirror, she swiped on a little bit of lip gloss. She already had a rosy glow to her cheeks thanks to rushing around her classroom all afternoon.

Amy carried her bags out to her SUV and climbed in. There was a chill to the air, which wasn't unusual for mid-November. She recalled how last Thanksgiving had been unseasonably warm though, with the kids forgoing their jackets on the playground.

Fifteen minutes later she pulled into the parking

lot adjacent to a row of shops in town. There was a bakery, which was just closing for the night, a small coffee shop, a used bookstore, and an art gallery. The gallery taught classes to the locals and had a small display area for people to purchase artwork. The coffee shop usually had a piece or two of the art on display as well, and the cross-promotion seemed to work well for the two small businesses.

Amy had always dreamed of owning the art gallery someday. She knew the couple in their mid-sixties that owned it wouldn't want to forever. It would be heartbreaking to see it close down if they were to retire. She certainly couldn't swing her mortgage plus rent for the gallery now though. Maybe someday if she saved up enough or managed to make money selling her paintings. Or if she ever rented out a room in her home. She wasn't too keen on that idea though—Amy enjoyed her privacy and alone time after being in a classroom full of children all day long.

Jason was already standing in the storefront when she walked up. He'd come straight from work and was in his dress uniform. Well, maybe it wasn't a dress uniform—it wasn't quite as fancy as what some of the Marines wore when they attended formal events. Melissa's ex-fiancé Michael, although not exactly her type, had looked incredibly dashing in his dress uniform. Jason looked equally handsome tonight though, his muscular frame accentuated by the cut of his uniform. His dark hair looked shorter than she remembered, but maybe he just looked more "military" now that he was standing before her in uniform.

Amy felt a slight flutter in her stomach as she approached him and wondered how he could have been living across the street from her all this time without her giving him so much as a second glance. Was she really that wrapped up in Ben these past few months? Sadly, she knew the answer was probably yes. When she'd been with Ben, she couldn't get enough of him, and even after they'd broken up, he'd been on her mind all the time.

It was amazing to finally have someone else she looked forward to seeing. Not that they were "seeing" each other. But the thrill that shot through her as she walked closer told her she wouldn't mind exactly that.

"Hi Amy, thanks for meeting me," Jason said warmly. "I'm sorry I wasn't able to get home in time to pick you up."

"Oh, it's no problem," she said, waving her hand in dismissal of his apology. "I had lots to do at school anyway and stayed late, so this was actually perfect timing."

"I'm glad it worked out then. Traffic around here is a nightmare. I felt terrible calling to say I couldn't pick you up."

"Jason, it's fine. And trust me, I don't mind driving anywhere if art is involved."

Jason laughed, gazing down at her with a twinkle in his blue eyes. "Good to know," he said smoothly. "Hey, how'd your bake sale go at school the other day?"

"Oh, really well. All my stuff sold out, and we made a ton of money for the preschool. Thanks for remembering."

"How could I forget? Those cookies were phenomenal."

"Thanks. The kids are already asking when we can hold another bake sale. I'm pretty sure I won't be up for that until spring at least. I've got enough to do with the holidays coming up."

Jason laughed. "It sounds a lot more fun than my day. Although I'm not sure what's worse, training a bunch of fresh-faced Marines or keeping a class full of preschoolers in line."

"Oh, the preschoolers are definitely more difficult. I could keep a roomful of Marines in line, no problem."

"You'd certainly hold their attention longer than I could," he added, his voice growing deep. "You're a hell of a lot prettier than me."

"Oh, you're not so bad," she teased. "Don't sell yourself short."

"My Marines would beg to differ," he said with a chuckle.

"Let's see if we can find you something inside," she said, shivering slightly.

"Lead the way," he replied, opening up the door and gesturing for her to enter first. "I didn't mean to keep us standing out in the cold."

Amy brushed past him as she walked inside, feeling her skin prickle and then go all warm over their closeness. He was so big and masculine, practically towering over her. As she caught a whiff of his cologne, it was all she could do to continue walking. If only she could stop there a moment, breathing in his scent and basking in his warmth. She could feel his eyes burning into her.

Jason stepped in beside her. "Hmmm, I'm not sure this is what I had in mind," he said with a low chuckle.

They looked around the room together at the pastel watercolors. The gallery frequently changed the theme of the pieces on display. Amy had stopped by several weeks ago, and the place had been filled with landscapes of forests and fall foliage. While that had seemed like it could be a possibility for Jason, the pastels were not at all what she could envision him enjoying.

"Darn it; they changed the display. It looks like they're featuring the work of an artist from DC right now. I'm surprised they don't have something more seasonal…." Her voice trailed off as she looked around.

Jason caught her eye and walked closer. "I'll have to check back another time then. How often do they change their display?"

"I'm not sure. Monthly? We could ask the owners."

"I definitely had something a little more modern or abstract in mind."

"Hmmm," Amy said, nodding absentmindedly.

Jason raised his eyebrows.

"I actually have something you may like. I hardly ever get the time to paint anymore, but I finished this piece over the summer. It's just sitting in my studio."

"Studio?"

"Spare bedroom, office, and studio all rolled into one," she said with a laugh. "Anyway, this piece I finished over the summer is just sitting there. I have so much art that I don't have the wall space for it. But I'd love for you to have it."

"I'd love to see it," Jason said. "Maybe I can stop by on Saturday to take a look?"

"Absolutely. I'd be thrilled if someone was able to enjoy it. I was just kind of playing around with abstract stripes, but it just might suit you. It's much more bold and modern than this," she added, gesturing to the pieces in the gallery.

"Yeah, I don't think I'm really a pastels kind of guy."

"What size painting were you thinking of getting?"

Jason suddenly glanced down, hands patting his uniform, and Amy wondered what he was looking for. Maybe he'd taken measurements of the different sizes of artwork he needed? Or had a list of ideas?

Nope, he was pulling out his cell phone.

\*\*\*

Jason's phone vibrated in his pocket, and he pulled it out, glancing down at the screen. He quickly scanned over the message his CO had just sent. "Damn it, it's work," he said with a frown. "I have to head back to base," he said quietly.

"Oh," Amy replied, her face falling.

He knew she'd been looking forward to enjoying the paintings in the gallery, and he'd hoped they'd even grab a drink or coffee afterward. Now their night was over before it had even begun.

"I'm really sorry," Jason said, holding her gaze. "I got stuck working late trying to wrap this project up, then I got stuck in traffic, and now I have to head back into work again to deal with this issue. This just isn't my night."

"I guess not," she said with a wry smile.

"Trust me, seeing you was the one highlight," he added with a laugh. "Brief as though it was. I feel terrible."

"Look, we all have days like that. Just come by this weekend sometime—if you're around."

"I'll be there," he promised, trying to reassure her. Did she think he was just bailing or something? God, he'd been looking forward to tonight for the past few days.

He glanced out at the darkening sky. "Let me walk you to your car before I go."

"You go ahead. I know the owners of the gallery, so I'll just stay and chat with them for a bit as long as I'm here. Good luck with the work stuff."

"Thanks. And I'm sorry again about this evening, Amy. Unfortunately, this is something out of my control."

He made sure she met his eyes before he said goodbye and left.

Jason felt horrible that he'd changed their plans not once but twice this evening. First he couldn't get home to pick her up and then he'd gotten called back to base. Of all the nights for something like this to happen. When was the last time he'd made any sort of plans with a woman? He sure the hell hadn't since moving here. The one night he had something to look forward to, his commanding officer had needed him ASAP.

Grumbling under his breath, he hurried back down the street.

The wind picked up, and he rubbed his hands together, trying to stay warm. He didn't even have a coat on, and the weather had turned decidedly colder since the morning. The cold blast of air made it feel more like winter than late fall, and if he didn't know better, it almost felt like snow would be headed their way soon.

He looked up at the darkening sky, almost expecting to see flurries. The scent of smoke from a fireplace nearby was permeating the air, and he wished he were headed to the comforts of home and not making the drive back to base.

Hell.

He'd love bringing Amy home with him—snuggling up by a roaring fire, enjoying a glass of wine. Finally seeing if she tasted as sweet as she looked.

At least he'd see Amy this weekend, no matter if it was just for a quick visit. He'd look at the painting she had and ask her out then on a proper date, he decided.

No more acting like he wasn't interested.

Saturday couldn't get here soon enough.

# Chapter 10

"So how'd the bake sale go?" Melissa asked the next night over dinner. She and Amy had decided to meet for a quick bite at a local Mexican restaurant. Melissa had spent the day taking a newlywed couple all over town looking for their first home. The fact that other people were still getting married and she wasn't had to be rough, and she'd called Amy late in the day pleading for a dinner companion.

"I spent all Sunday baking. *All* of it," Amy repeated for emphasis. "But the sale was a success, and the kids were thrilled. Now I've got to spend this weekend getting ready for Thanksgiving."

"I thought you were going over to Beth's with the rest of us?"

"I am, but I offered to bring a couple of pies," Amy replied, sipping her margarita. "What can I say? I must have been in a baking mood when I agreed to that. I need to get to the store, too—you know it's going to be crazy on Saturday morning with everyone doing their Thanksgiving shopping."

"I offered to bring the wine," Melissa said with a grin. "White, red, maybe a bottle or two of champagne…."

"You got off too easy," Amy jokingly scoffed. They all knew Melissa wasn't exactly known for her cooking. "And now they're saying that a snowstorm's coming. It seems really early in the year for that—you know how the weather forecasters are always predicting the next blizzard and then we only get an inch or two. But I may need to swing by the store tomorrow instead. If I'm stuck inside, at least I can get some prep work done over the weekend."

"Ugh—I hope it doesn't snow. The last thing I want is to sit around moping all weekend. Plus I have several showings, and this will mess up my schedule."

"You, mope?"

"Very funny. I've spent the last week cancelling all the vendors for my wedding. And the Saturday before that I spent with my ex-fiancé, yelling at him over the demise of our relationship. I was hoping for something a little more fun this weekend."

"Well, we'll all have a good time at Thanksgiving. And that's only a few more days away."

"I know; I'm just in a bad mood. Driving around town with that lovey-dovey couple did me in this afternoon." Melissa gestured to the waitress to bring another round of margaritas for the two of them. "Let's talk about you instead. Did you ever hear back from Ben after his ski trip?"

"God no. Why would I?"

Melissa shrugged. "You never know. Maybe he had a horrible time and wanted you back?"

Amy laughed. "I'm sure he had a terrible time on

his romantic vacation. All cooped up in that hotel room with a fireplace and king-sized bed. How about this—no more guy talk for the rest of the night?"

Melissa laughed and lifted her glass into the air. "That, my friend, is a promise."

\*\*\*

The commute home the next afternoon was horrible, with everyone else in the vicinity of DC leaving the office early as well. It had taken Amy an hour to make her usual ten-minute drive. The snow had been falling heavily all afternoon, and while there was an inch or two already on the grass, the roads and sidewalks were just beginning to accumulate precipitation. Finally reaching her street, she drove slowly down the road, leaving tire tracks behind in the wet, snowy mess.

After pulling into her driveway, she turned off her windshield wipers, and a thin layer of snow immediately began to cover the glass. She watched the snowflakes falling, one after another sticking to the windshield, until she could hardly see outside. Amy climbed out of her SUV and slid on the icy asphalt, clutching onto the side of her vehicle for support. Cursing herself for wearing flats today and not sensible boots, Amy pulled her tote bag, purse, and bag of groceries from the back of her car. She glanced down at the fresh white powder, which covered the ground in an even layer.

She slammed the tailgate closed and, heaving her tote bag over her shoulder, clutched the bag of groceries in one arm as she inched along the side of her car, heading for the front door. Confident that she hadn't fallen yet, Amy took a bigger step and suddenly slipped, falling backwards as she lost her footing.

Strong arms caught her from behind, and she cried out in surprise as she felt a firm body supporting her as she regained her balance. She looked up and right into the steel blue eyes of Jason. His hands remained on her arms as she steadied herself, and suddenly she felt flustered as he held her. How many times over the past few days had she imagined just this thing? Yet Jason pulling her into his arms and kissing her passionately was not exactly the same as catching her as she fell, and she realized it was silly to pretend it was anything more than him simply offering his assistance.

"Thanks," she said, turning to face him as he released her, noticing for the first time how tall he really was. She brushed some of the snowflakes from her hair and looked up at him.

"Are you okay?" he asked, his voice deep.

"Yeah, I just slipped in this icy mess," she said, gesturing to the ground.

"Those don't look like the best shoes for walking around in the snow," he said, eyeing her skimpy flats.

"Uh, no, probably not. I'm just coming from work. And I had to swing by the grocery store."

"Let me help you," he said, reaching out to take her things. He lifted her tote bag and slung it over his own shoulder and then reached out for the bag of groceries. As he held out his free arm to her, she saw no choice but to take it. Unless she wanted to walk up the driveway barefoot, she was going to have trouble navigating the icy mess in her shoes.

Gripping his muscular arm, she walked with him

to the front door. He towered over her, and she noted that he was well over six feet tall. She slipped once more but did not fall with Jason beside her, and she was grateful that he had been there to offer his help. She released his arm as soon as they reached the front porch.

"I'm surprised you had school today," Jason commented as Amy dug her keys out from her purse.

"The roads were fine this morning. I shouldn't have stayed late though. Traffic was terrible."

"For me, too. Nonessential employees were released early from base, but I think everyone else in the DC area was already on the road by the time I left. Took me two hours."

"That's terrible," Amy said, pushing open her front door. She pulled her key from the lock and walked inside.

Jason stepped in beside her. "Where do you want these?"

Once again, she felt a slight pang of sadness that Jason was just here for a moment. Of course he'd just come in to put down her things—it wasn't like they were about to spend a cozy evening together.

"Oh, just set them down anywhere. Thanks for your help."

"Sure thing. Let me know if you need any more assistance in the driveway," he said, a twinkle in his blue eyes.

Amy flushed, surprised that he was teasing her again. He always seemed so serious before and until the past week or so, they'd barely spoken. Something about all their unexpected encounters pleased her, and she smiled back up at him. "You'll be the first to know," she joked. "I'll just toss some pebbles at your window or something if I need help."

He laughed heartily. "Seriously though, if you need something, I'm right across the street. And I do want to see that painting."

"Definitely. Maybe you can stop by later on or tomorrow. I don't want it to get wet if you carry it home now in the snow."

"I can still come by tomorrow, if that's okay. Maybe you can come over afterward and help me pick out the perfect spot."

"Sounds good. Let's see if you like it first though."

He chuckled, the deep sound doing something funny to her insides.

"I'm sure I will, but even if it's the wrong colors or something, you're still welcome to come over for a drink. I have a feeling we'll be snowed in for a day or so with the horrible way they plow the streets around here."

"That I don't doubt," she agreed with a laugh. "And thanks again for your help. It would've been embarrassing to fall over right in my own driveway."

"You're welcome, Amy." The sound of his deep, masculine voice saying her name sent an unexpected thrill through her. Of course, he'd probably said her name plenty of times before. But something about her name on his lips and the memory of his arms around her in the driveway earlier made her yearn for something more. His gaze stayed on her for just a beat too long, and then he turned to go.

Her heart fell ever so slightly as she slowly shut the door behind him.

Walking into her bedroom, Amy pulled the shirt she'd been wearing over her head and slipped out of her wet jeans. Really, what had she been thinking not even bringing boots with her to school today? What if she'd gotten stranded on the road?

Pulling a stretchy camisole over her head, she then rooted around in her drawers looking for a cozy cardigan. Finding a soft cream one that hung open but was nice and warm, she slid her arms through, wrapping herself in comfort. She then grabbed a pair of black yoga pants. They were stretchy and comfortable, and she planned to spend the next few hours camped out at her kitchen table getting some work done before dinner. Thank God she'd already swung by the grocery store so she wouldn't have to go out again in this mess.

She walked into the kitchen, surveying the contents of her fridge. Aside from a mad dash through the store grabbing what she needed to make pies for Thanksgiving before the store shelves were empty, she'd picked up some of her favorite foods as a special treat: French bread and brie, which she never purchased, because who could eat that all by themselves, chocolate croissants for breakfast, and plenty of dark roast coffee, since she'd been running low. She had a roast and vegetables that she planned to cook tomorrow. Although that was a lot of food for one person, she'd freeze the extras and have plenty of meals for days. Plus, a nice roast in the crock pot reminded her of snow days when she was a kid, when her mom would have a meal cooking all day long, filling up the house with a delicious scent.

Amy sliced some bread and brie for a snack and put on a pot of coffee. She set her laptop up at the kitchen table while the coffee brewed and looked outside to watch the snow heavily falling. The streets were completely covered now, and she was glad that she didn't have to go anywhere else today. She poured herself a cup of steaming hot coffee and sat down, ready to get to work.

Several hours later she was still sitting there, typing up the newsletter she'd send out to the parents for the month of December. She was just starting to get hungry for dinner when the lights flickered a few times. Sighing, she rose from the table and walked over to the window in the dim evening light. Hopefully the power wouldn't go out. For now, the neighborhood was lit up with street lamps and the light coming from frosty windows. They were only expecting several inches of snow, but in this area, that could mean accidents all over the place.

She shivered, thankful that she didn't need to be anywhere else this evening.

Her phone buzzed on the kitchen table a little while later.

"Hey sweetie," came Beth's voice on the other end of the line. "How'd you do in the storm?" Amy could hear a male voice in the background and knew it was Nick. She glanced at the clock and realized that they were probably getting ready to sit down to dinner together. She'd need to find something to eat as well. Even though she'd planned a meal for tomorrow, dinner this evening hadn't been on her mind.

"The snow's starting to taper off," Amy said. "I've just been finishing up some work this afternoon. How about you guys?"

"We're going to try and find someplace open to eat because we lost power."

"Oh, that's too bad. Is your whole building out?"

"Yep. There's a crew outside working already, so hopefully it will be back on soon. Want us to come pick you up?"

"No, no," Amy said. "I'm fine here, and I don't want you guys to drive over in this mess. I'll talk to you later."

"Okay, bye hun."

"Bye."

Amy stood up from the table, ready to go raid her own fridge, when she heard the scraping of a shovel outside. She walked over to the window and was surprised to see Jason in her driveway. He had on a black ski jacket and black wool cap, and with the large shovel he was holding, had already cleared half of her driveway. She looked across the street and saw that his own driveway was clean as well, as was the sidewalk in front of his home. The snow had finally tapered off to a few flurries, and it looked like he'd made haste to get out there before nightfall.

She quickly pulled on her snow boots and warm red parka before heading outside to greet him.

"Hey there!" he called out. "I thought I'd quick shovel your driveway, too, before I go to Mrs. Jones's house."

"Wow, thanks. You really don't need to though. It's only a couple of inches; I can go grab my shovel."

"It's no problem," he said walking over to stand in front of her. "I'm almost done already. I'm not so much 'shoveling' as just pushing the snow off the driveway. Luckily there's not too much," he added with a grin.

"That's right—you're a California boy. You're probably not used to all this snow."

Jason laughed, his blue eyes sparkling. "Guilty as charged. What I'm really not used to is this crazy weather—I was jogging in a tee shirt a week or two ago. Now I'm out here shoveling snow? Something's wrong with that."

"It'll probably all melt tomorrow if this is all we're getting. The weather is always weird this time of year."

"I can see that," he chuckled. "And the forecast seems a bit off from the massive blizzard I was expecting. But I figured I'd help out a few neighbors as long as I was out shoveling my own driveway."

"Thanks," she said gazing up at him. She was half-tempted to invite him in for a cup of hot cocoa. He'd said he wanted to shovel the neighbor's driveway though, and she didn't want to prevent him from doing that since she knew her elderly neighbor really could use the help.

"You have some snowflakes in your hair," he said, reaching out to brush them away. She froze as he touched her, remembering what it'd felt like as he caught her in his strong arms earlier that day.

Had he felt anything, too?

Or was she just like the kid sister across the street that he was always coming to rescue? He was probably ten years older than her, but she *was* thirty-one years old. It's not like she was a child. So why was she always feeling so uncertain around him?

"So, I'll stop by in the morning to check out that painting?"

"Hmmm?" she asked, lost in her own thoughts.

"The painting. Is tomorrow morning still okay?" His blue eyes met hers, and she had the strangest feeling that he was leaving things unspoken as well. They were out in the middle of her driveway, but at that moment it felt like they were the only two people in the world. The street was quiet around them, covered in the softly falling snow. Everyone had come home early before the storm, and it was now dinner time, so there were no cars driving by or kids out playing. Amidst the soft white backdrop, it was almost like they were in their own magical winter wonderland.

"Yes, tomorrow morning's perfect."

"Great, I'm looking forward to it."

Amy wasn't sure if he meant he was looking forward to seeing the painting or seeing her again in the morning. "Me too," she hedged. "Are you sure you don't need any help out here?"

"No, I'm good. Go inside where it's warm. I'll head over to your next-door neighbor's house after I finish up here."

"Okay. Thanks again, Jason. I'll see you tomorrow. Have a good night."

"You too," he replied quietly, giving her one last glance before he turned away to continue working. She could have sworn that she saw that heated look in his eyes once more.

# Chapter 11

The doorbell rang at exactly eleven the next morning, and Amy pulled open the door to find Jason on her front porch, wearing his black ski jacket and jeans, and somehow looking sexy as hell. His hands were tucked into his pockets, and he'd stepped back from the doormat, like he didn't want to be too close when she opened the door.

He sure had that ruggedly handsome thing going for him, she thought as she met his gaze. He smelled of cologne and soap and something distinctly male, and she was dying to pull him closer, which was completely crazy.

"You look nice," he said, a smile tugging at his lips.

She flushed and glanced down at her pale pink sweater and jeans. Of course she didn't want to look like she was trying too hard. This was just supposed to be her neighbor dropping by to check out her artwork. But she had taken extra care this morning when she dressed, putting on a little makeup and selecting an outfit she liked. The lightweight sweater hugged her curves nicely, and the jeans were snug yet comfortable. All those hours running had paid off, so why not dress in something that made her look great, right?

"Thanks," she said, meeting his gaze again. "You too. I mean, come in," she said, stepping back and gesturing for him to come inside.

Jason smiled, and she wondered if he knew just how flustered she was around him. This was getting ridiculous. "Let me take your coat," she said. He shrugged out of it and offered it to her in a one-handed grip, and she noticed how muscular his hands were.

Briefly, she imagined them dragging over her bare skin, and then she decided she was being silly. They were going to talk about her artwork, not make out on the sofa like a couple of teenagers.

She nervously took it with both hands and hung it on the coat hook beside her front door. It looked perfectly in place right there next to her red parka, she thought with a smile. Not that he'd be over here all the time or anything, but still. It was a nice feeling having another man's things in her home.

My God, why on earth had she dwelled on her ex so long anyway?

"It looks like you were right," Jason said.

"About what?" she asked as she turned around.

"The snow is already melting."

Amy laughed. "Right, it's always like that this early in the season. We might get a snowstorm, but it's over almost as quickly as it started. Anyway, let me show you the painting. My studio is upstairs."

"Sounds great."

She turned, and he followed her up the stairs. It felt almost intimate leading him back toward the spare room, which was just across the hall from her bedroom. But all her artwork was in the small office/studio, so it seemed the most appropriate place to show him the painting she thought he'd like. She had a few others that could be possibilities as well if the one she had in mind wasn't exactly his style.

Jason entered the room and stopped beside her, letting out a low whistle as he caught sight of the painting she'd set out.

"Wow, Amy, this is amazing. Seriously. Are you sure you want to give it away?"

"Yes, of course. I paint a lot during my summer vacation and was just playing around with a more abstract piece. I have enough artwork on my own walls, and I'll be painting more once I have time off from school again. This one needs a good home."

"Well, at least let me pay you for it. I was planning to purchase a piece at the gallery."

"Oh, no, I couldn't accept anything for it. Maybe someday I'll open my own studio and charge you an arm and a leg then," she said with a grin.

Jason laughed. "Are you sure? I seriously don't mind."

"Absolutely. I have more art than I know what to do with at the moment."

"All right. At least let me take you out to dinner sometime to say thank you."

"Dinner would be okay."

"Just okay?" he teased.

"Dinner would be great," she corrected, glancing up at him. Their eyes locked for a beat, and for a split-second, she thought maybe he was going to kiss her. Her gaze fell on his full lips, and she felt heat rising within her.

The moment passed, and Jason gestured toward the painting.

"Why don't you come over and help me figure out the perfect spot for this?"

"Right now?"

"Sure, why not? We can see where it looks best and then have a drink or something. I seem to recall inviting you over yesterday. And I'd love the opinion of the talented artist herself."

Amy laughed. "Well, how could I turn that down? Flattery will get you everywhere."

He chuckled as he crossed the room. "I'll carry it over."

\*\*\*

"It does look good there," Amy said an hour later, admiring the artwork hung prominently above Jason's leather sofa. The blues and greens in the painting added a splash of color to the room. The rest of the neutral abstract stripes across the canvas simply blended right in.

He really did need decorating help, she thought as her gaze again swept the room. There were no pictures or paintings anywhere else, no knick-knacks lying around—just a cool, sparsely furnished space. Complete with a giant flat screen TV and surround sound, of course.

*Boys and their toys....*

"It looks incredible. You seriously don't know how much I appreciate it. Those watercolor paintings we looked at last week never would've done it for me."

Amy laughed. "Yeah, I realized that the moment we stepped into the gallery. Sorry about that."

"I'm looking forward to seeing what new pieces come in. Not that they'd be better than anything I saw of yours. Maybe you could do an art show there sometime."

"Maybe," Amy agreed. "I never really thought about it before."

"You should consider it. Seriously. Although I may regret that if you start charging me for your artwork from now on," he added with a wink.

She flushed, and then watched as he turned and put the hammer he'd been holding back in his toolbox. He snapped the lid shut and crossed the room, stopping right at her side.

Her skin prickled as he stood so near to her, and she imagined that he could hear her heart beating wildly in her chest. The heat between them was palpable, and she wondered how many times she'd imagined him pulling her into his arms. Did he feel it, too? That spark and connection between them each time they were in the same room?

She'd almost thought he was going to kiss her earlier when they'd been at her house, but he'd just been casually polite the entire time they'd been holding her painting up around his living room for the past hour. Now, with him standing so close once again, she wondered what he was thinking.

"Thank you again," he said in a low voice. "And thanks for letting me drop by this morning to pick it up."

She glanced up at him and smiled. Since she was in

her boots and Jason was barefoot, for once she only had to look up a few inches to fully meet his gaze. All he'd have to do was dip his head down ever so slightly, and those full lips would be on hers.

Kissing her.

Proving that there was some inexplicable chemistry between them.

She held his gaze a moment too long and then glanced over to the door.

When she looked back, his blue eyes were still firmly fixed on her. He hadn't made a single move though, and doubt started creeping in. "I should probably get going," she said, suddenly feeling flustered. "I'm sure you have other things to catch up on. Bye," she added hastily, turning to leave.

"Amy."

His voice was rich and deep. When he said her name, it wasn't a question or a command. The slow, smooth way that her name came from his lips was almost more like a caress.

She stopped and looked back, the electricity between them magnetic.

"Amy," he said again, softer this time, as he stepped in her direction.

She felt rooted to the spot, barely able to breathe, and her heart pounded in her chest as he walked closer. He didn't stop inches away like he had done before and hardly even gave her the chance to think straight. In the next moment his large hands were on her face, cupping her cheeks, holding her just so, and his lips were hot, desperate against hers.

He swallowed her cry of surprise, and she hungrily kissed him back, wrapping her arms around his neck, so that their bodies were pressed tightly against one another.

He tasted of mint and man, and as his mouth moved over hers, kissing her again and again, she felt dizzy with desire.

Desperate for more.

Her breasts pressed against his firm chest as they stumbled back together, and she felt his hard length against her stomach as he pulled her even closer to him. His hands slid down to her ass, and then he was lifting her into his muscular arms, her legs wrapping around his waist.

She gasped as his erection rubbed up against her core.

Heat coiled within her, spiraling down toward her center. Her nipples pebbled, every step Jason took jostling her against him. Leaving her whimpering for more.

\*\*\*

They clumsily fell back onto the sofa, Jason's large frame covering Amy's smaller one. Her lips were swollen from his relentless kisses, her face flushed, and he suddenly wanted all of her, now.

Needed to have her beneath him, moaning with desire, crying out his name.

He was aware that she was kicking off her boots, pulling him down closer with her small, delicate hands. She'd looked so damn nervous earlier, he'd wanted to pull her into his arms and assure her that yes, he wanted her, too.

Jason ran his hands down her sides, feeling her tremble, and slowly edged them beneath her lightweight sweater, pushing it up to reveal a black lacy bra.

God, was there ever a woman who *didn't* look sexy as hell in black satin and lace?

Amy put every other woman to shame though.

She was breathtaking.

The creamy skin of her luscious breasts poured out over the top of her bra, just beckoning for him to touch and caress. He felt dazed for a moment, staring at the woman beneath him. Did she have any idea how turned on he was right now?

He tugged one cup of her bra down, feasting on the sight of her bare breast. It was so round and smooth, with her dusty pink nipple pert, practically begging for his touch—suddenly he was impossibly harder, his erection straining against the confines of his jeans.

God this woman would be the death of him.

He cupped her full breast, squeezing it gently as she gasped, and then ran his thumb over her nipple, watching as it peaked under his touch. "God, you have perfect breasts," he said in a low voice, tugging the other cup down and watching them both rise and fall beneath his breath.

"Jason, please," she murmured, gazing up at him with wide eyes.

"I'll take care of you," he said huskily. He lowered his head to one breast, kissing and tasting until his lips were encompassing that softness and female perfection. He slowly kissed his way around her areola, savoring the moment, and she cried out as he flicked his tongue over her taut bud. Jason groaned in approval, sucking her nipple into his mouth, male pride filling his chest as she whimpered and squirmed beneath him.

He moved his mouth to the other breast and kissed and laved at her nipple. Oh, what he wouldn't do to hear those sounds come from her lips again and again. To have her begging for more. He lightly flicked his tongue across the nipple, teasing her, and she arched up off the sofa, completely at his mercy.

His hand trailed down her flat stomach, deftly unbuttoning her jeans and sliding the zipper down. He briefly registered her surprise at the ease he'd had, and a moment later she gasped as his fingers slid across the satiny fabric of her delicate panties.

Jason trailed thick fingers up her slit, feeling her arousal even through the fabric. She was so hot and wet for him already. He slipped a hand inside her panties, his sure fingers automatically knowing the way. A moment later he was easing through her slick heat, and he sucked in a breath at just how wet and aroused she already was for him.

His fingers slid through her silken arousal, circling her tiny bud, and she gasped again and arched her back, pushing her breasts up into the air. He silently groaned as he took her breast even further in his mouth. He suddenly was desperate to be inside of her. As quickly as possible.

But first he began to pulse his fingers against her sex, determined to finish what he'd just started—to unyieldingly make her come undone.

# Chapter 12

Amy gasped as Jason began to pleasure her. She hadn't been with anyone since Ben, and that was months and months ago. And although sex with Ben had certainly been good, she'd known him for practically a lifetime. There was a certain level of comfort she'd always felt when they were together. And comfort didn't always mean excitement.

Jason was practically a stranger compared to her ex.

A tall, sexy, Marine type of stranger.

He was new and mysterious; she'd known him for a matter of months compared to years. Now his muscular body was hovering over hers, his mouth was hot on her breast, and his fingers were working their own magic—and *damn*, did he know exactly what he was doing.

With each stroke of his fingers against her, Amy arched closer to him. The tension radiating through her felt magnificent—delicious and earth-shattering and unstoppable all at once. As the warmth began to spread through her body, she knew in only moments she'd be losing all control.

"I can't wait to be inside you," Jason said huskily into her ear, his breath tickling her with each word. His hand caressed and kneaded her aching breast, taking over where his mouth had just left off. "But maybe I should finish what I've started first?"

"Please," she whimpered, unable to give him more of a response.

"God, how I've wanted you," he ground out.

His strong fingers caressed her swollen nub, and he suddenly slipped two thick fingers inside of her, filling and stretching her for what was certain to come next. He worked them in and out, and she automatically thrust her hips to match his rhythm. His thumb slid back and forth across her clit, faster and faster, and a moment later Amy's cries filled the living room.

"Oh! Ohhhh! Jason!" she screamed, unable to contain herself any longer, as a surge of pleasure rushed through her.

He continued thrusting his fingers in and out as her inner walls clamped down around him, pulsing again and again. Her body arched up one final time and then collapsed back onto the sofa.

She panted as she looked up at him, the heat in his blue eyes scorching right through her.

"Oh my God. That was—I can't—"

Pure male satisfaction filled his gaze. "Honey, we're just getting started."

\*\*\*

They'd made love once right on the sofa, in such a hurry they'd barely had time to rip the clothes off of each other first. When they were finished, and after he'd managed to give her a second amazing orgasm, Amy had relaxed in the warmth of Jason's arms, sharing kisses with him in the waning afternoon light. As the day had given way to evening, Jason had lit a roaring fire and opened a bottle of wine. Content to relax together knowing that the hours of the night still stretched out before them, they'd talked and kissed in front of the flickering flames.

Jason had pulled his jeans back on and Amy her long sweater to ward off the chill, but she lay snuggled against his chest, inhaling his masculine scent and the hint of soap and aftershave she detected. She absentmindedly caressed the hard planes of his firm torso, practically in disbelief that they'd just made love right here in his living room.

Jason ran his muscular hands up and down her bare legs. She shivered in delight at the feel of his slightly calloused fingertips running over her bare skin.

"I kind of liked it better when you were wearing nothing at all," Jason whispered huskily, running his fingers farther up her bare thigh.

"And why is that?" she teased, trailing her fingers down his washboard abs so they just hooked under the waistband of his jeans.

"Ugh—you're killing me," he groaned. "But in the best, most erotic way possible."

She straddled his lap, kissing him slowly, and felt the bulge beginning to grow beneath his jeans.

Lowering her lips to his neck, she sucked gently, and Jason unwittingly began to gently thrust beneath her.

"Hmmm," she said, feeling his male hardness brush up against her sex.

She lowered her mouth to his shoulder, and as he reached around her, pulling her closer, the flash of his tattoo caught her attention.

Jason followed her gaze, and she slowly began to trace the emblem with her fingertips.

"Do you have a thing for guys with tattoos?" he asked, his voice gruff.

"I never did before…," she admitted. "But I have to say—it's kind of hot."

"Time to go upstairs," he said desperately, clenching his jaw as he stood up, lifting her to the ground as well.

"What's upstairs?" she challenged, knowing for the first time this afternoon that she was the one in control.

"A bed."

He took hold of her hips, guiding her closer to him, and in a moment his hot mouth was once again on hers. Their tongues intertwined and soon he was raising her sweater up and over her head and then desperately caressing her full breasts as she fumbled with the zipper on his jeans. They stumbled backward again, bumping into a low-back leather chair to the left of the sofa. "On second thought, this will do."

He gripped her shoulders and turned her around, bending her forward over the back of the sleek leather. He cupped her breasts as he stepped even closer, and her heart pounded in her chest. The leather felt cold against her bare skin and was in stark contrast to Jason's heated flesh. "Trust me," he whispered. She could feel his erection pushing up against her, and she felt a throbbing in her sex as she was suddenly desperate for him to take her.

He nudged even closer and kneaded her breasts with firm hands as he slid his erection back and forth through her wet folds. She groaned as the head of his penis brushed up against her sensitive bundle of nerves.

Jason gripped her hips in his strong hands, tilting her to meet him. The tip of his erection was pushing up against her wet entrance, and in one single, powerful thrust he was pushing inside her, filling her up with his immense girth.

She gasped as her inner walls clamped down around him. What had been amazing earlier was unbelievable in this position. Jason began to thrust inside of her, pulling her hips back to meet his every movement. She closed her eyes, lost in the moment as Jason took all control, filling her up again and again.

She was powerless bent over like this, and she gasped as he seemed to know just how to make her once again come undone. A moment later, his fingers slid to where their sexes joined, and she moaned as they teased her swollen nub. "That's it," he murmured, seemingly more to himself than her. He caressed her clit as his thrusts continued, and as the heat surged through her, she lost all control and once again screamed out his name.

Jason grew even harder and released as well, holding her to him as he gave one more final thrust. "Amy," he said reverently. "You have no idea how God damn sexy you are."

She lay panting and sated over the back of his chair, gasping for breath as he slowly pulled out.

Jason was breathing heavily as well, and she took pleasure in knowing she affected him as much as he did her.

He helped her stand up and then pulled her into his arms.

She collapsed against his muscular chest and let him hold her, still in a daze from the powerful orgasm she'd just had. There was no way sex with him—with anyone—could get any hotter than that. He knew just what to do and exactly how to please her.

And when his thick length filled her, she was lost to everything else but him.

She relaxed into his embrace, loving the feel of his skin against her own. Of his muscular arms around her.

A moment later, Jason tipped her chin up toward him, cupping her cheek as he gently bent down and kissed her lips. "Now let's go upstairs."

# Chapter 13

The next morning Jason blinked as he slowly awoke, feeling the warmth, soft skin, and curves of a woman nestled in his arms. Not just any woman though. *Amy*.

He smiled as he remembered making love to her in his bed last night. The sex in his living room was great, too, but he'd taken his time when they'd finally made it to his bedroom, wanting to show her just how much he cared. Her small body was tucked so neatly into his own this morning, it was as if she was made to be his. Male pride surged through him as he remembered her screaming his name as he pleasured her last night. What he wouldn't do to hear that every day. This moment was pretty damn perfect itself though. His head was beside hers, his arm across her, cupping one breast, and his growing erection was pushed up against her bare bottom.

Hmmm, he would have to do something about that.

Amy stirred beside him, and he whispered huskily

into her ear. "I could get used to waking up beside you every morning."

"Mmm hmm," she mumbled, turning over in his arms. "Me too. Oh," she said, glancing down at his hard length. "Looks like you're already awake."

"I couldn't help it. Amy, you are so damn sexy…." He rose up, balancing his weight on one arm, and leaned down to kiss her. She turned toward him, and he slid his hand across her chest, caressing and squeezing one breast. "Let's see if we can get you caught up…."

\*\*\*

An hour later, they'd both showered and dressed and were standing in Jason's kitchen. "I'm sorry I don't have anything better to offer you," Jason said, pulling frozen waffles from the toaster. "Next time I'll make you breakfast."

"These are fine," she said. "I have plenty of food at home anyway. I should've made you breakfast."

"Oh, I see. You're not here for breakfast, so you were just using me for my body last night." He flashed her a wicked grin, and Amy blushed despite herself.

"Hey, I'm just teasing," Jason said, walking over and planting a gentle kiss on her lips.

"I know," she said, pulling him back for another quick kiss.

He met her gaze for a moment. "I like having you here in the morning."

"I like it, too," she said, slightly surprised by her admission. Wasn't it just a week ago that she'd told her friends she was swearing off men for a while?

One amazing night, and she was suddenly singing a different tune.

Jason finished making the coffee as Amy glanced outside. She was happy to see the sun peeking through the clouds. "I wonder if the schools will be closed tomorrow," she mused. "I wouldn't mind a three-day weekend."

Jason looked toward the windows from across the room. "It doesn't look that bad."

"No, but trust me. They close the schools here for anything."

"The base will be open I'm sure," he said, his voice deep. He frowned as he opened the cupboards. In a way it felt like *just like that* he was back to business—back to the stoic, serious Marine he'd been before. She rather enjoyed the more playful side he showed around her. But of course tomorrow was the start of another week and back to reality for both of them.

Her cell phone beeped from the other room, and she went to retrieve her purse from where she'd left it yesterday afternoon.

As she glanced down at her phone, she saw a text from Beth.

*Power's still out!*

Amy thumbed a response.

*You guys want to come over?*

Her phone buzzed with a reply.

*Maybe later on. Heading out to breakfast now.*

Amy thought for a moment and then quickly sent her friend another message.

*Is it okay if I bring a guy to Thanksgiving?*

Beth's reply was immediate.

*Yes!!!*

Amy laughed at her friend's response as she walked back into the kitchen. A little over-eager, perhaps? She knew Beth just wanted her to be happy, though. Maybe it was a bit premature to be inviting Jason to Thanksgiving with her friends, but hadn't he just said he liked having her in his home first thing in the morning? If a guy was going to admit that, then certainly he would be okay with being invited to a friendly Thanksgiving dinner. It's not like she would be bringing him home to meet her parents or something.

Jason was setting two coffee mugs on the counter as she walked back into the room. "Everything okay?" he asked, glancing back at her.

"Yeah, that was just a friend of mine. She lost power in her condo yesterday, and they still haven't gotten it back."

"That's crazy. It's not even snowing anymore. Is she okay?"

"Oh yeah, she's fine. And as for the delay in restoring her power—well, that's life in Virginia for you."

"I hope everything gets back in order soon. Both for your friend's sake and everyone else around here. I need to get to work tomorrow and finish up a few things because I've got a plane to catch Tuesday afternoon."

"You're leaving?" Amy asked, her heart sinking.

"Yeah, I'm going to California for Thanksgiving. I'll be staying there a week."

"Oh," she said quietly, feeling slightly stunned and more than a little bit foolish. Why had she assumed he'd want to spend the holiday with her and her friends? Because she'd spent one night with him? It's not like they were dating.

Technically they hadn't even been on one single date. The night he drove her home from the restaurant was accidental, the evening at the art gallery was a bust. Did she really think that just because she'd slept with him, he'd forgo seeing his family in California and spend the time with her instead?

"So, do you take cream or sugar? Or just black?" Jason asked, turning toward her with a steaming cup.

"Just black is fine," she mumbled, reaching for the mug he offered without meeting his gaze.

"Everything okay?"

"Yeah, sure," she said, hoping he couldn't detect the hint of sadness in her eyes.

A moment ago, life had felt perfect, and now suddenly she just wanted to get out of there as quickly as possible. Not make any more of a big deal about sleeping with him than it really was.

"You know, I should probably get going," she said, setting the mug down on the table without even taking a sip.

"Go?" Jason asked, looking surprised as she turned back around. "But we didn't even have breakfast yet."

The uneasy feeling in her stomach was growing. If she didn't leave soon, she was afraid she'd start to tear up right in front of him. It was ridiculous, really. Why had she assumed anything at all? Just because they'd had one great night didn't mean he'd drop everything in his life for her.

Swallowing as she walked across the room, she refused to meet his gaze. "Yeah, I think it would be better if I just left."

"Look, Amy, if I did or said anything to upset you,

let me know," he said, catching her arm.

"No, it's nothing," she said, shaking him off as she walked down the hall and grabbed her coat from the chair. "Where are my boots?" she asked, frantically looking around.

"Amy, please," he said. "Tell me what's going on. Everything was fine a few minutes ago, and now you can't get out of here fast enough."

"I told you; it's nothing."

Jason sighed as she sat down and pulled her boots on. "Did something happen when your friend called?"

"Beth? No, she just texted me to see how I was. Well, I did ask her if I could bring a date to Thanksgiving dinner. But apparently, you'll be gone all week, so I guess there's no sense in inviting you. I shouldn't have assumed you'd be around—that was my own fault. It doesn't mean anything just because we slept together."

A flash of understanding crossed Jason's face. "Amy, I'm sorry. I made these plans months ago. Of course I'd love to spend the holiday with you, but I have to go to California. I promised my son I'd be there."

"You have a son?" she asked, staring at him in disbelief.

True, she didn't know much about Jason. He'd lived across the street from her for months and all she'd known was that he was in the military, polite, kept his yard neat, and drove a black sports car. But during the past few weeks she'd learned a few other things: he grew up all over the world, his parents retired to California, he liked to run, he drank his coffee black—he was amazing in bed.

But certainly *one* of the times they'd been talking and she'd slowly learned more about him he would have mentioned, at least in passing, that he had a *son*. Why would he keep that from her?

"Yes," he said, looking flustered. "I should have told you, but there just wasn't a great time to bring it up yet. I'm in this custody battle with my ex-wife—"

"You were married?" Really, the kicks just kept right on coming.

"Yes." He looked directly at her, his blue eyes intense. "When Kristin got pregnant, we decided to get married. We were never right for each other, and the marriage was over before it ever really began. But Brian, my son, has been living out in California with her. Now that I'm stationed in Virginia and not overseas, I'm hoping to get partial custody. It's all up-in-the-air right now. There's all this legal jargon that's extremely confusing, and it's frustrating for me to have Brian living on the other side of the country."

Amy stared at him, agape. "I can't believe it."

"I know I should have told you, Amy. Especially before yesterday. But I just wanted to straighten things out first with Kristin—finalize the custody, figure out where everything stands. I still don't even know what's going to happen. I might be the weekends and holidays dad until he's eighteen."

"You could have told me," Amy said, shock still reverberating through her body. Everything she'd imagined Jason's life to be was suddenly completely different. He wasn't just a single bachelor living all alone. He had an ex-wife. A child. He had a whole other life that she knew absolutely nothing about.

"I know; it's just been upsetting for me, dealing with all this. That's why I don't talk about it and hadn't found a way to bring it up yet. You've been a distraction from it all."

"A distraction." Tears welled in her eyes as she stood from the sofa. Here she thought their sleeping together actually meant something, and he was basically saying she was just a temporary reprieve from his *real* life.

Could this morning get any worse?

"No, I didn't mean it like that. You've been the one good thing about living out here. The one person I look forward to seeing. To hopefully dating. You don't know what it's like to never be able to see your own child. Someday when you have kids you'll understand."

"Someday when *I* have kids."

"Well, yes," Jason said, looking at her curiously. "You teach preschool. I just assumed—"

"I can't have children," Amy snapped, the tears rolling down her cheeks. "So yes, I understand unfairness and frustration. And you still could have told me. I mean you mentioned several times that you travelled a lot. Why not just say you were going to see your son? It's like you purposefully kept that information from me."

Jason looked shell-shocked and then seemed to come to and took a step toward her.

"Don't!" she shouted, holding her arms up to warn him to stay back. "Just don't."

"Amy," he said, his voice cracking slightly.

"I have to go," she said tightly. "Don't bother calling me again."

\*\*\*

Jason watched as she slammed his front door, wondering how the morning could have gone from absolute perfection to this.

One minute, Amy was waking up in his arms, in his bed, the next she was walking right out of his life. He rubbed a hand over his face, wondering if he should go after her. He was probably the very last person she wanted to speak with right now. Maybe he should just let her cool down and try to talk to her later on.

He'd really stuck his foot in his mouth, too. First with calling her a distraction and then by assuming she'd have children of her own one day. Obviously, she wasn't just a distraction to him. Hell, she was the best thing about living in Virginia, and he'd sure noticed her long before she'd given him the time of day.

And of course he'd assumed she wanted kids—she was a preschool teacher who loved what she did. He'd married Kristin when she'd accidentally gotten pregnant. Maybe it was naïve of him to assume every other woman would have it that easy, but what the hell did he know?

Leave it to his thoughtless remarks to hit Amy where it hurt the most.

Still, he wasn't sure how to fix the damage he'd just done. It's not like he could simply apologize for some mistake he'd made. Well, the "distraction" comment, maybe. But Brian would be in his life no matter what happened with the custody hearings. Amy could still never have children of her own. The question was, would Amy be able to accept any of that?

# Chapter 14

The next few days dragged on and on. Amy's students were all eager for the holiday, and they spent the week doing special activities. Her heart wasn't in it though, because she was too preoccupied over her weekend with Jason. She hadn't seen him at all since Sunday morning. He'd tried calling her despite her protests not to and had even tried knocking on her door one evening. She'd refused to answer, and he'd eventually just gone back home.

She knew he was gone for real now, out in California for his Thanksgiving vacation. Nothing was worse than heading to work every morning and seeing his empty house across the street. If this wasn't a good reason to never get involved with a neighbor, she wasn't sure what was. In the future she'd have to only date men who lived far, far away.

On Thanksgiving morning, she rose early and baked the promised pies for her friends. Normally she enjoyed baking, but for once she wished she'd taken on Melissa's job of just picking up a few bottles of wine. The last time she'd spent hours in the kitchen she'd even carried over a plate of cookies just for Jason, she remembered sadly.

That afternoon Amy sat down with her friends to a spectacular meal. Beth and Nick had outdone themselves with a wonderful roasted turkey and stuffing, mashed potatoes, gravy, sweet potatoes, green bean casserole, and cranberry sauce. Kara and her husband Aaron had brought over some amazing appetizers for everyone to snack on before the meal, Melissa had brought an entire case of wine, and Amy had baked four different pies. She probably didn't need that many for their small group, she realized, but everyone could take leftovers home to enjoy tomorrow.

"Bethie, you outdid yourself," Nick said when the meal was over. The group sat around the table in Beth and Nick's condo, sipping on their wine and occasionally glancing over at Kara's twin girls sleeping beside them. Miraculously, they'd gotten both of them down for a nap just before dinner, so Kara and Aaron were able to enjoy their meal in peace and quiet. It was a small break that Amy was sure the two of them appreciated.

"Thanks, hun. Next year, you're in charge of Thanksgiving dinner though."

The group all laughed, and Nick looked around sheepishly. "Hey, I helped with all the grocery shopping. And I did an awesome job chopping onions and celery for the stuffing."

"Top notch," Aaron agreed with a laugh. "Now how are you at preparing baby bottles?"

Everyone laughed again. "That, my friend, is one

job I'll leave to you," Nick said. "That and the whole changing of dirty diapers."

"Oh God," moaned Melissa. "And to think Michael and I could have been where you guys are next year. It's awesome that you're so happy, but I was *this close* to marital bliss and just like that Michael took it all away from me."

"Have you heard from him?" Amy asked.

"He actually called me this morning, believe it or not. We were supposed to have Thanksgiving at his parents' house this year, so I imagine he's still there. His mother probably guilt-tripped him into calling me. I hadn't heard a thing from him since that afternoon he came over to my place. Remember when I was late to our girl's night?"

The rest of the girls all nodded. Amy thought maybe it would have been better if she hadn't asked Melissa about him. It turned out she should have just changed the subject from men completely, because the next thing she knew, Beth was asking her about Jason.

"So why didn't you bring him along?" she asked, lovingly caressing Nick's arm and tilting her head toward him as she looked over at Amy. "He would have been more than welcome—I told you that."

"Wait—bring who?" Melissa asked, glancing over at Amy.

"No one," Amy replied in the same moment that Beth answered "Jason."

"Jason?" Melissa asked, puzzled. "Wait—JASON Jason?"

"Who's JASON Jason?" Aaron asked, confused.

"Don't know but that's an unfortunate name," Nick quipped.

"All right, why don't you two make yourself useful and start clearing the table," Beth hinted. "The rest of us are in need of a little girl talk."

"Yeah, yeah, we can take a hint," Nick begrudgingly joked, getting to his feet. He picked up his and Beth's plates and stacked them together. Aaron gathered the rest before following him into the kitchen.

"All right," Melissa said after they'd cleared the room. "You've been holding out on us, so SPILL. When were you planning on inviting that man over for Thanksgiving dinner and more importantly, why didn't you?"

"It's nothing," Amy said firmly, shaking her head. "I asked Beth if I could invite someone to Thanksgiving dinner, and I didn't."

"Well why not?" Melissa asked disbelievingly. "That man was hot!"

"He wasn't honest with me about a lot of things," Amy said with a shrug. "He wasn't who I thought he was."

Beth was the only one she'd told about Jason. She of course had asked who Amy was bringing to dinner, and the whole sad story came out. Amy made her promise not to tell the others because she just didn't feel like reliving it all over again. Yet now, here she was, having to explain away something she was hoping to keep buried.

"Well what happened that he wasn't honest about?" Melissa persisted.

"He's married."

"Married?" Melissa asked, aghast.

"Divorced," Beth clarified.

"He's divorced, he has a son—he has an entire life

that he never even mentioned to me. Not that I know him that well, but he came over during the snowstorm to look at my paintings, and one thing led to another…."

"You slept with him?" Melissa shrieked.

"Shhh!" Amy chastised as one of Kara's babies began to wail.

"You slept with him?" Melissa whispered.

"One time."

"One time or one night?" Melissa asked, jokingly waggling her eyebrows.

"I'm not answering that. The next morning, he said he was really happy that I was there. Beth happened to text me and that's when I brought up inviting him." She shrugged. "It doesn't matter. He already had plans, so I didn't invite him. You know what? I'd rather just forget about it. Let's talk about Kara's girls or what time we're having dessert, or the weather, or *anything* else. How's that?"

Beth smiled sympathetically from across the table, while Kara was distracted by the wailing from one of her twins. Melissa looked a little hurt and disappointed that she'd been left out of learning the whole story, but Amy just didn't feel like discussing any of it right then.

And while Melissa had always been happy to share what happened in the bedroom with her ex, there was no way Amy was sharing anything about her night with Jason.

Not even with her best friends.

She'd put the whole thing behind her and would try to forget the feeling of Jason's muscular arms holding her close or his hot lips all over her body.

Or his hard length buried deep inside her while she

cried out his name.

    She'd try to think of something, *anything*, but that.

# Chapter 15

Amy knew he was back when his car disappeared from the driveway one morning. The long holiday weekend was over, and life had returned to normal. Or not exactly normal, since she hadn't spoken to Jason in over a week, ever since she'd stormed out of his house Sunday morning.

Or maybe life was back to the "Pre-Jason" normal. It's not like she'd spoken to him much at all when he'd first moved here. A wave hello here, a 'good morning' there. She could go back to that someday.

Maybe.

The snow had long since melted, and the kids had been bouncing off the walls on their first day back at school. So was she, truth be told. She felt anxious and antsy now that she knew Jason was back in town, and she was certain that she was bound to run into him at some point.

What was she supposed to say?

The hurt and regret she was feeling made just the

idea of seeing him unbearable right now.

Amy turned her attention back to the classroom, saying goodbye to the students as the last parents and caregivers trickled in to pick them up. She had a lot to catch up on after the Thanksgiving holiday but was hoping she'd be able to get in a late afternoon run before heading home.

Her mind drifted, thinking ahead to the next few weeks. Before she knew it, Christmas would be here. Although the girls had gone out the morning after Thanksgiving, the malls had been so crowded, they'd shopped for only an hour or so before retreating to the safe haven of a restaurant for lunch.

Kara was excited for her twins first Christmas, and Beth was on cloud nine for the first Christmas she and Nick would have together in her condo. Amy and Melissa were the only ones not bursting with excitement. It would be nice to have someone to spend Christmas with, but for the first time in years, Amy would be alone.

Of course she'd go home to her parents' house in Maryland, so it's not like she'd truly be alone. Hopefully her sister would be there as well, but Amy never knew what her sister's schedule would be like while she was completing her residency.

Amy changed into her running gear before heading out from school, slipping on a warm fleece over her tee shirt and pulling on a fleece headband and gloves. Carrying everything out to her SUV, she climbed in and drove over to the parking lot she preferred to use for running on the trails.

It was amazing how much the landscape had changed in just a few short weeks. The leaves had all fallen off the trees, the cold air had the smoky scent of winter to it, and even the sky was gloomy and gray as if announcing that winter was indeed here.

Although she didn't particularly care for cold weather, she didn't mind running in it. Running was a distraction and a way to clear her head of everything else. Nothing else mattered as she pounded on the trail through the forest.

Nothing and no one.

She smirked, realizing the last time she'd come here she was upset about Ben. How silly that seemed now. If Jason had done one thing for her, it was to help her finally get over her ex.

Now if only she could find a way to get over Jason as well.

\*\*\*

Jason pulled his son's suitcase from the trunk of the car the following weekend. The little boy stood beside him, glancing around and looking both excited and nervous at the same time. Although Jason's enjoyment of Thanksgiving weekend had not been without a dark cloud hanging over him due to the way things had ended with Amy, his actual visit to California had gone off without a hitch.

He'd gotten to see his parents and brother, he and Kristin had finally reached a custody agreement without needing a court hearing, and perhaps best of all, she'd agreed to let Brian spend the two weeks before Christmas with him. He'd had to make arrangements at work to rearrange his shift, but it was all well worth it to spend quality time with his son. Now here they were, a week later, standing in his driveway together.

They'd always bonded when he'd gone out to visit, partly because he'd travelled to be with Brian so much. He'd also been lucky in that his and Kristin's wasn't a bitter divorce. She'd always allowed him access to Brian, even when she maintained full custody, and Brian had grown up knowing as much as he could of his father, even though Jason had been stationed on the other side of the world.

He still hadn't seen Amy since he'd returned, and he hadn't figured out the right way to smooth things over. Now that his son was visiting it would be even more awkward to go over there. He would've loved for Amy to meet Brian, but now certainly wasn't the right time.

Not when she was still upset with him.

And hell, he still hadn't even gotten to take her out on a proper date. No wonder she thought he was a first-class jerk. He hadn't told her about Brian. He'd slept with her and then made her feel like he wasn't interested in anything more by leaving town almost immediately after. By offhandedly saying she was a distraction.

He still felt crushed every time he pictured her face before she'd run out the door—the hurt and sadness had been unmistakable.

"Are you sure this is Virginia?" Brian asked, glancing up at him questioningly.

Jason laughed as he looked down at him. "Of course I'm sure. What makes you ask that?"

"Well, it doesn't look any different from California."

"Maybe not," Jason agreed. "What were you expecting?"

"I don't know. Maybe some different trees and

grass."

"Different trees and grass," Jason chuckled. "These do look pretty much the same," he said, glancing around. He noticed Amy's car was gone from the driveway and wondered if she was out running errands this morning. The last Saturday he'd been in town, Amy had come over to see the painting and spent the night in his bed.

In a single moment, he'd managed to screw things up so badly she wanted nothing to do with him. Now there was a definite possibility that he'd run into her since he'd likely be in and out all day with Brian. He was nervous to see her again, not knowing how she'd react.

Jason had gotten up early this morning to drive to Reagan National Airport to pick up Brian. Jason's brother had been home on leave over Thanksgiving and was able to accompany Brian on the cross-country flight. It had been good to both pick up Brian and give his brother one last goodbye before he returned to duty. R&R was never long enough, but it had been nice that his brother had been able to make it all the way home this year.

"What do you say we head inside? I'll show you the tent I set up for us to camp out in the living room."

"With sleeping bags?" Brian asked excitedly.

"Yes, two sleeping bags. One for me, and one for you, buddy. Next time I'll have a bed set up for you—promise."

"No, sleeping bags are better!"

"High five?" Jason asked.

"High five!" Brian shouted, jumping up in the air.

At that exact moment, Amy's SUV came driving

down the street. Jason cringed slightly at the bad timing. She'd obviously seen him standing in the driveway with Brian, and now here he was just staring at her.

He felt a slight twisting in his gut as he caught a glimpse of her behind the wheel. This wasn't the right time for him to rush over there and convince her they needed to talk. It would be rude of him to not at least wave hello though. As her car approached, he raised a hand and waved. It was a friendly, neighborly gesture, if not exactly the way you'd want to greet the woman you'd just slept with.

The woman who'd stormed off in tears.

Hell, maybe he should've sent her flowers and written a note of apology. Tried harder to get her to talk to him.

But now?

He was standing here with his son, left to do nothing but watch her return home.

Her car pulled into her driveway and she stepped out, wearing those running tights again and a fleece jacket.

"Who's that?" Brian asked. "Do you know her?"

Jason realized he was still staring, and Amy glanced over in their direction, her brown ponytail bobbing with the turn of her head. She had dark sunglasses on, so Jason couldn't see her eyes, and her mouth was set in a tight line. She nodded ever so slightly at him as she went to the back of her SUV to retrieve her grocery bags from the trunk. If she hadn't needed to walk in that direction, Jason had a feeling she wouldn't have even acknowledged him at all. Not that he deserved any different.

"Why didn't she say anything? I saw her looking at

us."

"Doesn't matter," he said, putting a hand on Brian's back to guide him inside.

"Why?"

"It's just grown-up stuff."

"Like what?"

"She's mad at me right now. Now come on."

"Are you mad at my Dad?" Brian shouted across the street.

"Brian," he said firmly, giving him a stern look.

Amy looked back at them, startled, her rosy lips forming a perfect "o." Jason felt his chest clench as he looked at her. Hell, he wanted nothing more to go over and take her into his arms. Beg her to forgive him. Apologize for making her feel the way he had.

Now wasn't the time for any of that though.

"Sorry," Jason called over, his voice gruff. He was still holding Brian's suitcase, and Amy had two bags of groceries in her arms. He knew Amy wouldn't yell or get mad at him in front of his child, but this wasn't exactly the way he planned to smooth things over.

He needed to look into her eyes and apologize, not call out from across the street.

"I have to put my groceries away," she said, her voice halting. She bit her lip and turned, walking quickly toward her front door.

Jason felt his heart breaking all over again. "Let's go inside, buddy," he said, looking down at Brian.

"I don't think she likes you," he said in his little four-year-old voice.

"You know what? I think you're right. I made a mistake and need to apologize. But right now, we've got to get you settled in."

He led Brian toward his front door, grumbling

under his breath. Amazing how he could be elated to finally have his son here and so damn sad at the same time.

# Chapter 16

Amy felt the tears welling in her eyes as she hastily shoved her keys in the front lock. She jiggled them around while balancing the groceries in her arms, and then nudged the door open with her knee when the doorknob finally turned.

She'd been expecting to run into Jason at some point but hadn't considered she'd be forced to get out of the car and unload her things while he and his son stood there and watched. It was humiliating, really. He had a life already, filled with plenty of people and plans for the future, and there was certainly no room for her in it.

Not when he'd never mentioned his child to her in the first place.

Carrying her groceries into the kitchen, Amy thought back to the summer, when she and Ben had just begun dating. God, she had noticed Ben for years, always wanting to be around him with his charisma, good looks, and charm. After just watching from the sidelines as he dated girl after girl, he'd taken notice in her when he returned to town last spring. When they'd finally gotten together it had been like a dream come true.

Then out of nowhere, she'd discovered she was pregnant. She and Ben both had been nervously excited. She was on birth control pills but there'd been that one time she'd forgotten to bring them on a weekend away, and they hadn't been able to stop themselves. That was all it had taken, and in an instant she'd been planning a life revolving around her child.

When she'd lost the baby a month later and found out she could never have children, it had been devastating. They hadn't told anyone that she was pregnant, and just like that they'd kept the loss a secret as well. She'd broken up with Ben shortly after that, unable to deal with the heartache. Ben moved on with his new girlfriend, now fiancée, perhaps trying to heal in his own way.

That Jason had a son didn't bother her as much as that he'd kept it a secret. And then when he'd said she wouldn't understand until she had a child of her own was like a dagger straight through her heart.

She sighed, tossing some of the pre-packaged cookies she'd bought onto the counter. She hadn't meant to blurt out that particular piece of knowledge to Jason. Hell, even her best friends didn't know. But there had been such a raw anger rushing through her at the moment, she'd wanted to say something, anything, to make him understand the hurt.

And now it looked like Jason had won whatever custody battle he'd been fighting with his ex-wife since his son was visiting. It's not like she was about to move away, so she'd just have to get used to it.

Suck it up and watch the man she'd slept with having fun with his son.

It was a one-night-stand. A mistake. Not the start of a relationship. It didn't mean anything.

In the meantime, she only had a couple of hours to get ready for her friends to arrive. She was throwing a tree-trimming party this afternoon, and she still hadn't even gotten her tree up yet. Although picking out a fresh tree sounded appealing, she had an artificial one in the basement that would just have to do for this year.

On second thought, maybe she could turn her tree-trimming party into a tree-*assembling* party as well. Since the guys would be here with her friends, she figured Nick and Aaron could help her lug it upstairs to the living room. She still needed to shower and change and then get snacks and drinks ready for her friends. Maybe putting on a little Christmas music would get her more in the mood.

She walked over to her mp3 player and turned it on, hearing the strains of a Christmas tune just ending. She'd had her playlist set to holiday music all week, attempting to cheer herself up. It wasn't the same though without Christmas decorations filling her home.

This afternoon with friends was just what she needed. A few decorations, some music, drinks, and the scent of spiced cider filling her home might be just what she needed to get back in the holiday spirit.

\*\*\*

"Hey!" Jason called out as Amy's friend got out of

her car later that afternoon. The wind whipped through the air, and she wrapped her arms around herself in an attempt to stay warm. "Hey, Red!" he shouted more loudly.

She turned in the direction of his voice, a puzzled expression on her face. Her eyes narrowed and she put both hands on her hips as he jogged across the street toward her.

"Red?" she asked accusingly as he got closer.

"Yeah, sorry," he said as he came to a stop in front of her. "I don't know your name; that's just how I think of you."

"So you think about me and not…say…Amy? And it's Melissa, by the way."

Jason smiled, shaking his head. Obviously, Amy had told her friends what had happened, and they weren't going to make it easy for him. "Not in the way you're thinking of, honey."

She laughed and then seemed to remember that she was angry with him. "So why are you running across the street to see me? Amy lives right there."

"I need your help," he admitted.

"And I would help you because…?"

"Because I hurt Amy. I didn't mean to, and I just need to talk to her to apologize and explain myself. Even if she doesn't want to see me again, don't I at least owe her that?"

Melissa tilted her head to the side as she appraised him, "Look, I don't know if it would make any difference. As far as I know, she thinks you're a total jackass."

Jason winced at that, knowing that Amy had every right to be angry with him. Melissa seemed to take pleasure in passing on that particular bit of news to him, but he realized she was upset for her friend's sake.

"Look, just put in a good word for me if you can. Please tell her that I would love a chance to explain myself. Yes, my son Brian is here for two weeks, as you can see," he said, gesturing toward his house, where Brian was watching from behind the glass storm door. "But if you could at least ask her to answer the phone when I call…. I don't want to keep bothering her, but I can't stand knowing I've upset her this much."

Melissa considered his plea. "All right—I'll try," she said shortly. "I can't promise anything though."

"Thank you," Jason said, nodding appreciatively. "And please, just tell her that I'm sorry. I didn't mean for any of it to happen the way that it did."

"Okay," she said with a shrug. "I'll see what I can do."

She turned back to her car and retrieved her purse and a bag teeming with garland, ornaments, and tinsel. He eyed the bag questioningly. "Tree-trimming party," she explained. "Amy loves Christmas."

He nodded, an idea suddenly coming to him. "Good to know. Thanks again for your help," he said, turning away. He jogged back across the street and pulled open the door, scooping up Brian into his arms. Even if she didn't want to see him again, he wanted to apologize. Make it right. And beg her to give him another chance.

\*\*\*

"Like this?" Nick asked an hour later, trying to arrange the lights according to Amy and Beth's direction.

"No, you're missing that whole section," Beth protested with a laugh. She good-naturedly tossed a strand of garland at him that was waiting to be hung next, and he easily snatched it out of the air.

"Hey! You're teaching the girls how to misbehave!" Kara chided. She and Aaron were sitting side-by-side on Amy's sofa, feeding each baby a bottle.

"I don't know that they'll remember this," Amy said with a laugh. "Now, when they're toddlers though, that'll be a whole other story."

"We won't bring them to a tree-trimming party then," Kara said. "They'll break everything!"

Amy shook her head and laughed. The tree was standing in her living room, the boxes of ornaments were scattered about, and her friends filled the room with easy banter and laughs. She hadn't had this much fun in a while. Actually, the last time she'd enjoyed herself so much was that Saturday with Jason—before all hell had broken loose the next morning. As mad as she was, she actually missed him, she realized. It's too bad he'd turned out to be such a jerk.

She was a distraction from the rest of his life?

Whatever.

"What are you smiling about?" Melissa asked, nudging her as she appeared with two mugs of spiked eggnog.

"Truth be told? I was wishing Jason hadn't turned out to be such a jerk."

"He came over to see me on my way in here."

"What?" Amy asked, practically spitting her eggnog back out.

"Don't care, huh?" Melissa asked with a laugh.

"Now *Michael* was the real jackass this year. We were engaged to be married, and he completely broke my heart. Jason may have bumbled around in the way he did things, and he should have told you about his son. But he cares about you. And apparently, he's been trying to talk to you?" she asked, raising her eyebrows.

"Yes, before he left," Amy said, clarifying the matter. "But I haven't heard from him since. He's moved on, and that's all that matters now."

"I did it!" Nick called out from across the room. "Now *this* is definitely better. Amy? Please tell Beth that I can climb down from this step-ladder now." He was balancing atop her short step-ladder, the end of the lights wound right to the top of the tree, ready for the star. If she could find it.

"Yes, it looks great!" she called back. "Let the man down, Bethie!"

"Not you, too," Beth said, jokingly rolling her eyes in reference to Amy's use of Nick's nickname for her.

Melissa leaned over, and Amy met her gaze. "He hasn't moved on," she said quietly. "If anything, I think he's quite smitten with you. And quite desperate to get you to speak to him again."

Amy looked at her, puzzled, as Melissa set her eggnog down and walked away, grabbing the silver garland she'd brought. "I know this is for the tree, but it looks so much better this way, doesn't it?" she joked, wrapping it around her shoulders and doing a little shimmy as she crossed the room.

"Maybe you should give up real estate and become a Vegas show girl," Beth said with a laugh.

Amy smiled, too, but glanced past the tree, out her front window. Jason and his son were in the front yard, and she watched as Brian happily shrieked while Jason chased him around the yard.

Her heart ached, and she realized that as much as she loved being here with her friends, she wished she were right out there with him.

# Chapter 17

Jason's car was still in the driveway every morning when she left for work, and Amy wondered how long he was taking off and for how long his son was staying. Through Christmas? That seemed unlikely since his mom was supposed to retain primary custody. Or so she thought. Maybe he was here for the week.

When she arrived home later that evening Jason's car was finally gone but there was a small, wrapped present sitting on her doorstep. Puzzled, she picked it up. There was no card attached, and she carried it inside to unwrap it. As she tore off the paper, she noticed some writing on the small cardboard box. In black marker, it simply said:

*This made me think of you.*
*Jason*

Suddenly feeling very curious, she opened the box to see a Christmas ornament nestled inside. Pulling it out, she saw that it was a small snow globe, and as she looked closer, she was shocked to see the art gallery she and Jason had visited. The whole row of shops on Main Street was there—the coffee shop, bakery, bookstore, and art gallery, each with tiny details painted on and their names in small letters.

When had Jason found this? *Where* had he found it? He didn't seem like the type to go shopping for sentimental gifts. He knew she loved the gallery, and it had been their first and only "date" that really wasn't.

She swallowed, feeling moved that he'd found this for her. Melissa had talked to Jason the day of her party. Had she told him that each of her friends had brought over a special ornament? Or was it just a coincidence?

She was amazed he'd taken the time to pick out something that she'd really love. Walking into her living room, she hung it on the tree. The glass reflected the lights, and the snow globe shook, the snow softly falling to the ground as it settled back into place. She heard a car door slam a moment later and saw Jason walking around to the passenger side. Suddenly feeling brave, she decided it was now or never, and she marched out the door and across the street.

Jason looked startled to see her. He helped his son out of the car and introduced them, and Amy couldn't help but smile as the little boy shook her hand. "We're just getting back from the park," Jason explained, his voice deep. "It was a little cold, but we had a fun time."

"And we saw a deer!" Brian shouted. "A real one!"

"Wow, that is very special," Amy said. "I wonder if it was a reindeer."

"A reindeer?! Daddy! She said it was a reindeer!" Brian shrieked happily, jumping up and down.

"Maybe so, buddy," Jason said with a chuckle. He looked back to Amy, his blue eyes bright and alert.

"I just wanted to say thank you for the ornament," she said softly. "I love it."

"I knew when I saw it that it was perfect for you," Jason said with a warm smile. "I only wish I could've given it to you in person."

"Yeah, well, thanks again," she said as Brian raced around them. She watched him for a moment then looked back to Jason. "I guess I should get going. You guys just got home."

"Wait, Amy. Can I come by later on? I really need to talk to you."

"I don't think that's such a good idea," she said hesitantly.

"Please? Can I at least call you? Tonight? I won't keep bothering you, but I really just want to explain myself."

Her heart fluttered in her chest as she looked up at him. This could only end badly, and although logic and reason were telling her *no*, do not agree to talk with him, her heart was screaming *yes*. "Yeah, I guess so," she said hastily, turning again to go. "Bye," she called back over her shoulder as she walked down his driveway.

Jason grinned and looked down at his son. "Come on—I'll race you to the front door!"

\*\*\*

That evening Amy nervously paced back and forth in her living room. Waiting for Jason to call was *unnerving*. Besides, what if he didn't even bother? He was wrapped up taking care of his son this week—she got that. She wondered what time four-year-olds went to bed and then realized the little boy was still probably on west coast time. It would be a while before she heard from Jason.

Amy showered and changed into her pajamas, deciding to settle in with a movie for the evening. If she heard from Jason—great. And if she didn't, then she'd just gotten her hopes up for nothing.

She walked over to her Christmas tree, admiring the snow globe ornament that he'd given to her. It was perfect, and she was touched that he'd thought of something to give her that he knew she would love. She curled up on her sofa, pulling a warm blanket over her. Flipping through the TV channels, she finally found a Christmas movie to watch. The only thing better would be a hot cup of cocoa—*that, and someone to drink it with*, she thought with a wry smile.

When the phone finally rang half an hour later, she actually jumped in surprise. She'd been so into watching her movie that she'd actually forgotten about Jason's call—was that a good or a bad thing? Now she was a bundle of nerves all over again, and her heart raced as she answered.

"Hello?"

"Amy. Hi. It's Jason." He seemed nervous as well. She didn't recall him ever sounding so disjointed before.

"Hi," she said softly.

"Sorry I wasn't able to call sooner. I just got Brian off to bed."

"I figured you'd be busy with that."

"Yeah, the poor kid hasn't adjusted to the time

change. He's here visiting for two weeks though, so as soon as he gets used to Eastern Standard Time, I'll have to send him back to his mom," he said with a low chuckle.

"So I guess you worked out a custody arrangement?"

"Yes, we did," Jason said, sounding more and more like himself. "He'll be able to come visit me every month—at least for now while he's young. We'll have to work out a whole new arrangement when he starts elementary school in a couple of years, but we'll cross that bridge when we get to it."

"Well, I'm glad it worked out for you," she hedged.

"Thank you." He paused for a moment, and she knew he was about to bring up their fight and the weekend they spent together. Their conversation up to this point was just pleasantries, but they both knew the reason he wanted to talk. "Amy, listen, I feel terrible that things happened the way that they did. I mean, I never expected that weekend to happen at all. I wanted to take you out to dinner, drinks, get to know you—I'd been hoping to ask you out that night at the art gallery, but I got called back to base. And I never meant to keep the fact that I had a son from you. I honestly just hadn't had a good chance to sit down with you and talk."

"I know," she said with a sigh. "I just—I just felt like you intentionally kept it from me. And then you told me how I couldn't understand—" her voice broke off and she fought back the tears that once again threatened to fall. No matter what Jason had or hadn't said, it didn't change the stark truth—in a way she couldn't, *wouldn't*, ever understand, because she'd never be able to have a child.

"Amy," Jason said, his voice thick with emotion. "I'm so sorry."

She sniffed but didn't answer as fat tears rolled down her cheeks.

"Please don't cry."

"I should go," she sniffled, wanting to end this call as quickly as possible.

"No—wait. I'm coming over," he decided.

"Now? I'm in my pajamas. And what about Brian?"

"I'll be right over."

The line clicked as he hung up the phone and Amy stared at it, dumbfounded. Did they really need to talk about this right now and in person? She'd agreed to talk over the phone, and that seemed like a nice way to ease back into things. She wasn't sure if she was ready to forgive him yet even though a part of her desperately wanted to.

Just like Melissa had noticed, Amy saw how amazing he was with his son. It was impossible to find fault with that—if anything, it was just the timing of the situation that had gone all wrong. And as for the comment about having children—who hadn't asked her that? She was a preschool teacher—everyone assumed she wanted and would have kids.

A moment later a knock came at the door, and she hesitantly went down the hall. She'd changed earlier into her red flannel pajamas. They were warm and cozy but not exactly what you'd wear to have a man over for the evening. She cracked the door and saw Jason standing there in the cold, wearing cargo pants and his black ski jacket. "Jason, look, this really isn't a good time. I'm in my pajamas!"

"I don't care," he said firmly. "I'm so sorry that I hurt you. Can I please just come in?"

The pleading look in his eyes made her hesitate, and a moment later she opened the door further. Jason stepped inside, the cold radiating off him as he entered. "Whew—it's freezing out there tonight. Can I take this off?" he asked, gesturing to his jacket.

"Fine," she said crossing her arms across her chest. She felt a little ridiculous standing there like that, but he was the one who'd insisted on coming. "Where's Brian?"

He nodded at her neighbor's house. "I asked if she could watch him."

He shrugged out of his jacket and hung it from the front doorknob. Glancing into her living room, he saw the Christmas tree in the front window. "Your tree looks good there," he said, his voice deep. One beat passed, and then two. Finally, he turned back toward Amy. She nervously licked her lips as he gazed at her, and he cleared his throat. "Please tell me how to fix this," he said quietly. "I'd give anything to take back what I said."

Tears filled her eyes, and although she'd sworn to herself that she wouldn't cry when he came over, they slowly spilled down her cheeks.

"Please don't cry," he said huskily, taking a step closer to her. They were still in the front hallway, and Amy took a step back, finding herself with no place to go as she backed against the wall. She wiped the tears from her cheeks. "Please don't cry," he repeated.

He was right in front of her now, cupping her face in his hands and wiping her tears away with his thumbs. "Amy," he breathed, leaning down so that she felt his breath on her cheek, "I'm so sorry."

He slowly kissed the side of her face, kissing each tear away. As he kissed his way across her forehead, she closed her eyes, and in a moment he was gently kissing the tears off of her other cheek.

"Please forgive me," he whispered, trailing his fingers gently up her neck and entwining them in her hair.

She tilted her head up to meet his gaze, seeing the devastation across his face. She'd never seen him look so vulnerable before—Jason was this big, tough Marine, always seeming so strong. Would he look so upset if he didn't care for her? "I'm sorry, too," she said. "I shouldn't have gotten mad at you."

He dipped his head down, tightening his grip in her hair, and slowly kissed her. Amy kissed him back, running her hands up his muscular chest and locking them behind his neck. Jason deepened the kiss, his tongue edging inside her mouth, tasting and discovering her there. When they finally came up for air, Amy was gasping against the wall. Jason lowered his mouth to her neck, softly kissing and tasting before allowing his teeth to gently graze across her skin. "Let's go upstairs," Amy said breathlessly.

Without even giving a response, Jason bent and scooped her up into his arms. He slowly ascended the stairway, staring deep into her eyes and even ducking down for another kiss as he held her close. The layout of their homes was exactly the same, and Jason turned, instinctively knowing the way to the master bedroom at the end of the hall. He carefully laid Amy on the bed and then paused a moment, eyeing her meaningfully. "I can't stay all night—not tonight; I've got Brian."

"I know," she said, reaching out to pull Jason to

her. "It's okay."

He bent down, kissing her softly as he slowly unbuttoned her pajama top. As he undid each button, he kissed her flesh, slowly working his way down her chest and abdomen. When he finally reached her stomach he looked up, pushing her top open to reveal her breasts. "Amy," he breathed, softly kissing the underside of one breast as he worked his way up to her nipple. He took it into his mouth, sucking and flicking his tongue lightly back and forth across it.

Amy felt a fluttering in her lower abdomen and a surge of moisture beneath her pajama bottoms. As soon as Jason removed them, he'd see just how hot and ready for him she was.

He moved to her other breast, planting heated kisses all over before taking that nipple into his mouth. He lightly tugged on it with his teeth before teasing her further with his tongue. "Oh!" she gasped, feeling the pleasure shoot straight through her.

Jason pulled his shirt up and over his head, and once again she admired his wall of muscles. He was pure male perfection, and right now he was doing all that he could to please and satisfy her.

He unbuttoned his pants, pulling them down along with his boxers. His thick erection sprang out, throbbing with need, and she reached down to assist him in taking her own pajama bottoms off. Jason kissed her stomach, working his way down lower and lower until she was practically trembling with desire. He hovered over her center but then kissed her inner thigh, slowly working his way up until at last his mouth was above her core.

"I want to taste you," he said huskily, giving one long lick up her center. He gently parted her lower lips with his thumbs and bent to softly caress her throbbing clit with his tongue.

She gasped and lurched up off the bed.

If she thought Jason was amazing in bed before, it absolutely paled in comparison to the pleasure he was giving her now. Warmth was surging through her, and she could swear she was beginning to see stars.

He expertly tongued and laved at her arousal dampened folds, leaving her fisting the sheets as she moaned. "Jason," she gasped, as she thrust her hips closer to him.

"I've got you, baby," he said, giving her a couple more ministrations with his tongue before sucking her clit between his lips.

She exploded and shouted his name, pleasure coursing through her entire body. He gently continued licking her, allowing her to slowly fall back down to earth. "That was unbelievable," she panted, meeting his heated gaze.

"I'll never get tired of hearing you scream my name," he said gruffly, kissing his way back up her body until at last their tongues intertwined once more. He slid a finger to her entrance, teasing her a moment before gently thrusting it inside. He added a second finger, stretching her, as his thumb slid over her clit.

She whimpered and he pulled his hand away, positioning himself above her. A moment later, he slowly inched his hard length inside.

Amy groaned as he filled her up, inch by amazing inch. He moved slowly this time, seemingly in no hurry, and that made it all the more pleasurable and simultaneously unbearable. She wanted him—now. She needed him to soothe the ache building deep inside of her, to thrust deeply into her and give her release.

Jason slowly ground into her, and she wrapped her arms around him, moaning his name. His hips worked their own magic, allowing him to penetrate her deeply as he repeatedly rubbed the base of his erection up against her swollen clit. She gasped, and just when she thought she could no longer bear it, he sped up, powerfully thrusting into her until she was clinging to him and crying out his name.

He finished as well, shouting his own release, and collapsed on top of her, burying his face into her neck.

They lay there like that for a moment in the darkness, Jason still inside of her. "I don't want to leave you," he said sadly.

"I don't want you to either."

He finally pulled out and bent down to kiss her. "Mrs. Jones is watching Brian. I said I'd be back in less than an hour."

"It's okay—just go. We'll see each other soon."

Jason kissed her once more and then slowly got dressed. Amy pulled on her robe to walk him out, and Jason took her hand as they went to the front door. In a flash she realized they'd kissed and had sex plenty of times, but they'd never done something as simple as hold hands. It felt nice. As they reached the front hall, Jason raised her hand to his lips. "I'll call you in ten minutes, okay? I just need to thank Mrs. Jones for watching Brian."

"What did you tell her anyway?"

"That you were upset and I needed to talk to you."

"She already thinks we're a couple."

Jason raised his eyebrows. "How so?"

"That night you drove me home from the

restaurant—she spotted you standing in my driveway."

Jason grinned and bent down to kiss her again. He pulled on his jacket and went back out the front door. Amy smiled as he left, actually looking forward to his call this time. She went into the living room and turned off the TV that had been left on all this time and folded the blanket back up.

A few minutes later there was a knock on the door, and she wondered what Jason had forgotten. She opened the door and was shocked to see him standing there with his sleeping son in his arms. Amy stepped to the side and let them walk in, watching Jason carry Brian over to her sofa. He'd been wrapped in a blanket, but Amy added the one she'd been using earlier as well to make sure he stayed warm.

"I can't believe you came back," Amy whispered, guiding Jason over to the kitchen so they wouldn't wake Brian.

"I didn't want to leave you," he said sincerely, his blue eyes bright with emotion.

Amy smiled and stood up on her tiptoes, running her hands over the dark stubble on his cheeks and pulling him close for a kiss. Jason wrapped his arms around her waist and smiled down at her. "So I know we still haven't gone out on a proper date yet…but Christmas is only two weeks away. What should I get you?"

"I don't need anything for Christmas" she said, shaking her head. "Just you."

"A Marine for Christmas," he mused, a gleam in his eyes.

"That sounds perfect to me."

"Done," he said with a grin. "There is one more thing I was wondering though…."

"What's that?"

"Are you wearing anything under that robe?"

Amy laughed and grinned up at him. "Nope."

"I may have to check this out for myself," he mumbled, ducking his head down for a kiss.

"So don't I get to ask what you want for Christmas?" Amy said between kisses as Jason guided her toward the stairs.

"I don't need anything either."

"Nothing?" she teased.

"Nope. I already have you."

# Author's Note

Thank you so much for reading ONE NIGHT WITH A MARINE! Melissa's story is next in the series. Find out what happens in HER SINFUL MARINE.

If you're a new reader, be sure to also check out my Alpha SEALs series.

Sign up for my newsletter so you never miss out on a new release.

As always, thank you for joining me on this writing adventure. I wouldn't be here without you!

xoxo,

Makenna

# About the Author

Makenna Jameison is a bestselling romance author. She writes military romance and romantic suspense with hot alpha males, steamy scenes, and happily-ever-afters.

Her debut series made it to #1 in Romance Short Stories on Amazon. Makenna loves the beach, strong coffee, red wine, and traveling. She lives in Washington DC with her husband and two daughters.

Visit www.makennajameison.com to discover your next great read.

# Want to read more from MAKENNA JAMEISON?

# Keep reading for an exclusive excerpt from the second book in her Sinful Marines series, *HER SINFUL MARINE*.

Melissa Ford is done with men. Especially the tall, handsome, and military kind. After being burned by her ex, the last thing she needs is a new man in her life. Especially her cocky, arrogant, and smoking hot new client. With broad shoulders, muscles to die for, and an ego a mile wide, he spells nothing but trouble. The sexy and sinful kind.

Marine Corps Sergeant Tyler Braxton needs a new place to live. And the sexy little redhead that's showing him properties around town. Melissa has porcelain skin and curves that won't quit—not to mention a sassy mouth that has a comeback for every single one of his lines.

When Melissa goes missing one weekend, Tyler will stop at nothing to make sure she's found safe and unharmed.

But it will take a hell of a lot more to convince her to be in his bed—and his life.

**Her Sinful Marine, a standalone novel, is book two in the Sinful Marines series.**

# Chapter 1

Melissa Ford blew out a sigh, impatiently tapping her stiletto as she waited for her new client to arrive. She glanced down at the time on her phone, mentally calculating how long she'd have to spend showing him the house before she had to rush off to her next appointment. Weekends were always the busiest for her, with back-to-back showings of properties. She understood why people preferred seeing homes on Saturday or Sunday, but this was *her* work. She didn't have time to waste on late arrivals or no-shows who couldn't even bother to tell her they weren't coming.

She walked across the porch, her heels clicking on the smooth stone, her gaze sweeping the empty street.

Not a car in sight.

So much for doing her best friend a favor. She never took on new clients first without a preliminary meeting in the office to go over everything. And this was exactly why.

Serious inquiries only.

Perching on the wrought-iron bench, she crossed

her legs, the skirt of her slim suit tightening across her thighs. She worked out occasionally—nothing like her best friend, who was an avid runner—and her outfit today skimmed her curves like a glove. Amy always had said she'd kill for Melissa's hourglass figure.

Not that Melissa minded flaunting her assets.

She adjusted her suit jacket, the camisole she had on beneath hugging her full breasts. At least it wasn't ninety degrees out in the summer or something. Then she'd really be irritated. Still, she had better ways to spend her day than sitting around on the front porch of a house she needed to sell. Not when she had other showings back-to-back.

Other people waiting for her.

Melissa tried calling her client again, on the off-chance that he'd gotten lost.

In a car accident.

Attacked by zombies.

She smirked, brushing her long red hair back over her shoulder. The phone rang and rang but then went to voicemail.

Tyler Braxton had been stationed clear across the country somewhere in Colorado and had only recently moved to Quantico. He'd been renting but was looking to purchase a house here. She'd never even met the man, only dealt with him via phone and email. And maybe she never would meet him, she thought, annoyed. If he couldn't be bothered to show up or cancel, she'd move on to her other clients.

She should've known better than to agree to meet with the Marine. Her own ex-fiancé certainly had turned out to be unreliable, what with proposing to her and then up and cancelling the wedding only two months before the big day.

Guys like that were married to their careers.

Or interested in sleeping with as many women as possible.

Why should Michael tie himself down to her when there were plenty of other fish in the sea?

She smirked.

Three years wasted with him. Although Amy was happily dating her neighbor, Jason, who happened to be stationed at Quantico as well, he seemed to be the anomaly.

The rest of them were all assholes.

Fifteen minutes later, a large black SUV pulled up to the curb, and a burly Marine who had to be none other than Tyler stepped out. He was at least six-foot-two, with cropped blond hair and aviators concealing his eyes. Broad shoulders were proportionate to his thick biceps, straining against the sleeves of the polo shirt he had on. It was tucked into cargo pants, and she could see he was all muscle as he moved toward her.

Melissa blew out an irritated breath and stood, striding across the front porch. She didn't miss the way his gaze swept appreciatively up her body. Or the hint of a smile tugging on the corner of his mouth.

Typical.

Guys like him probably thought women would fall at their feet everywhere they went.

Heck, maybe they did.

But she'd done that song and dance already. She

sure the hell never planned to date a man in uniform again. He could be the hottest Marine ever to walk the face of the Earth and she wouldn't give him a second look.

Besides, with her long red hair and feminine curves, she was used to men staring at her. Watching as she walked past. Hinting that they'd love to take her out.

She primly held out her hand in greeting as Tyler jogged up the steps to the front porch, and suddenly his muscular hand was clasping around hers, holding it just a beat too long.

"You're late."

His eyebrows raised as he pulled off his aviators. "Apologies, ma'am," he said, his striking green eyes sweeping over her with interest. "I couldn't get my date to leave."

"You had a date at ten on a Saturday morning?" she asked in disbelief.

"No. She was still here from last night," he added with a smirk.

"Well, isn't that lovely," she said, turning and walking back across the porch. She could feel his eyes on her ass as she walked, and she resisted the urge to swing her hips. Like she needed his type as a client.

Good grief.

"I would've appreciated some notice," she said. "I was about ready to leave. I've got back-to-back clients scheduled today."

He chuckled. "Jason said you were a handful."

She glanced over her shoulder to glare at him. "I'm doing Amy a favor by showing you this house.

Normally we need financials, preapproval from your lender—the whole nine yards. We sit down and go over everything in the office. And normally my clients are courteous enough to arrive on time, not spend the morning in bed with their one-night-stand."

She fiddled with the lockbox as he came to a stop behind her, and she tried to ignore his clean, masculine scent. Or the feel of his large frame hovering behind her. She could feel the heat radiating off his body, despite the slight chill in the spring air, and realized she liked it a little too much.

Which was ridiculous. So he'd showered and put on some aftershave before he came over. Big deal. He clearly didn't have an ounce of common courtesy.

And he was already seeing someone.

What type of woman he spent the night with, she didn't even want to know. Tyler had said his "date" wouldn't leave, but he didn't exactly seem like the dating type. More than likely, he'd picked up a woman at one of the bars in town and brought her home. Then tried to rush her out the door this morning.

Typical man.

She slid the key into the lock a moment later, and then she was pushing open the front door. Striding across the sleek wooden floors, her stilettos clicking with every step.

Tyler paused in the entryway, watching her as she glanced back at him. His broad shoulders filled the doorframe, and she forced herself to keep her eyes on his. "You're supposed to be looking at the house, not me."

He chuckled and gazed around. "Gorgeous."

She bristled slightly, wondering if he was referring to her or the home. Not that it mattered. He'd already pointed out that he'd been late because he was having sex with someone. Good grief. "It's three bedrooms, two and half baths," she began, running through her usual spiel. "Move-in ready, as you can see. On a third of an acre. The owners were military also and just moved out. It's going on the market first thing Monday morning."

"Why are you waiting until then?"

"I'm having professional photos taken tomorrow, and then it will be listed."

Tyler strode across the empty living room, pausing in the door to the kitchen. "It might be more space than I need as a single guy, but it's a good investment. There's enough transition in the area with military and contractors coming and going all the time. I don't imagine I'd have trouble selling it in the future."

"Absolutely. Houses around here move quickly, as you know. The entire DC area market is hot right now. If you see something you're interested in, it won't be available for long."

He smirked. "Same with women. If I see someone I want, I go for it."

Melissa resisted the urge to roll her eyes. Was he really coming on to her? After admitting he'd been with a woman last night?

"That's lovely," she said, pasting a fake smile on her face. "Would you like to see the rest of the house?"

"Absolutely. Ladies first," he said, gesturing toward the stairs. The deep rumble of his voice sent a thrill shooting straight through her.

Ridiculous.

All his silly little innuendos were just to get under her skin.

She turned and walked ahead of him, tossing her long red hair over her shoulders. Determined not to let him rattle her. Goodness. Amy and Jason owed her big time after this. She hadn't expected the friend of Jason's from base to be more obnoxious than her ex.

And Michael had never acted like that when they were together. It was only after he called off the wedding that he'd turned into a total jackass.

"You seem rather different than Amy," Tyler commented. "She's a preschool teacher who loves running, and you're—"

"What?" Melissa asked breezily. "Out of your league?"

He chuckled. "Prancing around in stilettos. Wearing short skirts to show homes."

She smoothed her snug skirt absentmindedly as she took another step. It was snug, meant to accentuate her curves, but short? Not exactly. Her stiletto heel caught on the carpet just then, and she wobbled slightly, clutching onto the railing. Tyler's large hands landed on her hips, his broad chest at her back, and she resisted the urge to gasp.

Briefly, images of his muscular body moving behind her flashed through her mind. Positioning her how he wanted. Claiming her as his own as he whispered naughty fantasies into her ear.

Which was absurd.

Stiffening as she regained her footing, she cleared her throat. Took a purposeful step away from Tyler. "Amy teaches preschoolers," she said as she reached the landing. "I don't think suits and stilettos go with finger paint and playdough, do you?"

"Not exactly. I just expected someone more like her. Although Jason did warn me about you, don't get me wrong. I guess I should've taken his word for it," he added with a laugh.

"And pray tell, what did Jason say?" she asked. She tilted her head to gaze up at him, seeing the glimmer of amusement in his green eyes. Even with her sky-high heels, he still towered above her. She was right in line with his broad shoulders. He was entirely man and muscle—a force to be reckoned with. Cocky with the goods to back it up.

And she'd nearly fallen over on the stairs right in front of him, for heaven's sakes.

It wasn't like her to let a man rattle her so. Especially a client.

"I believe ball buster were the words he used," he said, those full lips quirking into a smile as he gazed down at her "I nearly fell off the barstool laughing."

"Why, did you have a few too many? You look like you should be able to hold your liquor."

His deep laughter filled the empty house. "Do I look like the kind of man who follows a woman around, dick in hand? I told him not to worry, I could handle anything you throw my way. As a matter of fact, I think we can work together just fine."

"Shall we move into the bedroom?" she asked innocently, turning and leaving him standing there at the top of the stairs.

<u>Available in Paperback!</u>

Made in the USA
Monee, IL
31 October 2019